"And so you are stuck with me."

"Nay, I am not stuck, Jedidiah Lapp."

Her answer delighted him, and he studied her fondly. He would like the memory of the evening to take home to Happiness with him.

He held out his hand, and Sarah looked at it a moment before their fingers touched as she accepted his help onto the wagon seat.

"All set?" he asked, and she nodded. "Are you cold?" She shook her head. "Are you going to be silent during the entire ride?"

"Nay," she said with what sounded like horror.

He laughed. "I am teasing you, Sarah Mast."

He saw her lips curve before her laughter joined his.

"Shall we take the long way home?" he asked, expecting her to decline.

To his surprise, she said, "You are the driver."

He drove at the slowest pace he could manage. He would enjoy this time with her; having her on the seat next to him was enough to keep him happy.

He didn't like the thought of leaving her, of never seeing her again, but what could he do?

Books by Rebecca Kertz

Love Inspired

*Noah's Sweetheart
*Jedidiah's Bride

*Lancaster County Weddings

REBECCA KERTZ

has lived in rural Delaware since she was a young newlywed. First introduced into the Amish world when her husband took a job with an Amish construction crew, she took joy in watching the Amish job-foreman's children at play and in swapping recipes with his wife. Rebecca resides happily with her husband and dog. She has a strong faith in God and feels blessed to have family nearby. She enjoys visiting Lancaster County, the setting for her Amish stories. When not writing or vacationing with her extended family, she enjoys reading and doing crafts.

Jedidiah's Bride

Rebecca Kertz

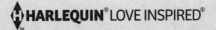

Recycling programs
for this product may
not exist in your area.

™ LOVE INSPIRED BOOKS

ISBN-13: 978-0-373-81763-4

JEDIDIAH'S BRIDE

www.Harlequin.com

Printed in U.S.A.

Stop and consider the wondrous works of God.
—*Job* 37:14

For Evan…for believing.

Chapter One

❧

Late May, Kent County, Delaware

"Sarah! Are all the baked goods in the buggy?"

"*Ja, Mam.* I put them carefully on the backseat." Sarah returned to the large white farmhouse where Ruth Mast stood inside the front screen door. "Everything is ready to go."

"*Gut,*" Ruth said. "Iva will keep me company today. Mary Alice will help you at the Sale."

Sarah nodded without argument although she knew that the day would be eventful with two wild boys to mind at the Sale. She worried about her mother, who had been feeling unwell for some time. Her *mam* hadn't been out of the house except for Sunday services for months. Aunt Iva had taken *Mam* to the doctor's last week, but *Mam*'s refusal to share the results of that visit frightened Sarah.

A black buggy drew up and parked in the barnyard, and Iva Troyer and her daughter Mary Alice stepped out of the vehicle.

Sarah waved a greeting to her aunt and cousin as she searched for signs of her brothers. "Timothy! Thomas! Time to go to Spence's!"

"Coming!" a young voice cried.

The boys came barreling around the house. Their straw hats flew off as they bolted toward the buggy, revealing twin mops of bright red hair. Her brothers looked disheveled as they halted before Sarah, out of breath.

"Boys! Your hats! Get them and quickly!" Sarah narrowed her gaze as her brothers obeyed and then approached. "You clean enough for town?" she asked, examining each with a critical eye.

"Ja," Timothy said as he jammed his hat back onto his head.

"Only our hands are a little dirty," Thomas added, "but they don't look it."

"Nee, they are clean," Timothy insisted. "We washed them in the pond."

"Let me see." The twins stuck out their palms for her inspection. "You've been playing with frogs again," she guessed, and saw Timothy nod. "Go wash your hands with soap." She kept her smile hidden as they scampered toward the house. "And comb your hair!"

The boys weren't gone for long. "Bye, *Mam!"*

they cried in unison as they raced by their mother and out of the house.

"In the buggy, boys!" Sarah instructed. "And don't touch the baked goods." She turned to lock gazes with her mother. "I'll make them behave."

Her mother managed a slight smile as she opened the screen door and stepped outside. "I know you will, daughter," Ruth replied as she watched her youngest sons scurry into the buggy.

Sarah hesitated as she eyed her mother with concern. *Mam* wore a royal-blue dress. The dark color emphasized Ruth's sickly pallor. The white *kapp* on her head hid the gray in her dark hair.

"She'll be fine," Iva assured her. Iva Troyer, *Mam*'s sister, was a large, strong woman with a big, booming voice.

Sarah nodded. As she hugged her overly thin mother, she gave up a silent prayer. *Please, Lord, make* Mam *well again.* She caught her aunt's glance and relayed her silent gratitude. Iva gave her a slight smile as she steered her inside the house to rest.

"My *mam* will take *gut* care of *yours,*" Mary Alice said as she climbed into the Mast family buggy.

"I know she will." Sarah joined her cousin in the front seat. Mary Alice was tall but thinner than Iva. She wore a green dress without an apron, and a white *kapp* over her sandy-brown hair. "I appreciate your help today."

Mary Alice shrugged. "I like going to the Sale. I'm getting a barbecued-pork sandwich for lunch."

Sarah smiled, grabbed hold of the leathers and then steered the horse toward Dover. "Sounds *gut* to me."

Early morning at Spence's Bazaar was a beehive of activity as vendors and folks set up tables with their items for sale and prepared for the crowd that the warm spring day would bring.

Jedidiah Lapp arranged brightly painted bird-houses, stained and varnished shelves and other well-crafted wooden items on his uncle's rented table. He set some of the larger things, such as side tables, trash boxes and potato bins, on the ground where potential customers could readily see them. Finished, he turned to review his handiwork.

"Looks fine, Jed." Arlin Stoltzfus joined him after a visit to the Farmers' Market building across the lot. "Here." The older, bearded man smiled as he handed his nephew a cup of coffee, and Jed nodded his thanks. "You finish unloading the wagon?"

"Ja," Jedidiah said. "Almost everything you brought today is out and ready to be sold." He reached into a cardboard box beneath the table to pull out two cloth nail bags. *"Dat* gave us these to hold the money." He handed one to his uncle.

"Your *vadder* is a wise man," Arlin said as he stuffed dollar bills and coins into the bag's sewn compartments. "Where are all of your *mudder*'s plants? I don't see many."

Jedidiah shrugged before he adjusted his straw hat. "I put the rest under the table. I can put out more later after we sell these."

"Nee," Arlin said. "We'll put more out now." He shifted things about to make more room for his sister's plants. "Your *mam* will be hurt if we don't sell everything she gave us."

Jed smiled. "We'll sell them." He helped his uncle rearrange the plants before he reached beneath the table to withdraw more of his mother's plants. "The sage look healthy."

"Ja, and the vegetable plants are thriving." Arlin looked pleased by the new display.

"Mam's kept busy in her greenhouse ever since *Dat* and Noah built it for her."

Arlin grinned. *"Ja."* He lifted a hand to rub his bearded chin. "She gave me ten tomato seedlings and four green-pepper plants," he admitted. "And she says she'll have more for our vegetable garden next week."

"You've got a fine selection of wooden items." Jed admired his uncle's wares.

"Enough, I think." The older man moved a trinket box to the front of the display.

Jed agreed. Arlin had crafted enough items to stock several shops back home in the Lancaster area, including Whittier's and Yoder's Stores. He'd spent weeks building birdhouses out of scrap lumber donated by the Fisher wood mill. Besides trinket boxes, he'd built hanging shelves that he'd carved and painted, vegetable bins, side tables and fancy jewelry boxes that would appeal to *Englischers*. Arlin had hospital bills to pay; his daughter Meg had suffered from some health issues. His Amish community in Ohio had held fund-raisers to help with Meg's medical expenses. Once Meg was well, Arlin moved his family to Happiness, where his sister lived. While he was grateful for his new community's help, Jed's uncle felt it was his responsibility to pay off the remainder of his debt. Someone had told him that he'd sell a lot of his handiwork at Spence's Bazaar Auction in Dover, Delaware.

Jed set down his coffee cup. "We're all glad you decided to move back to Happiness, Arlin." Their village of Happiness was in Lancaster County, Pennsylvania.

Arlin's stern face warmed with a smile. "I'm glad, too. Missy's *mudder* and *vadder* can't understand why their daughter converted to Old Order Amish. They are *gut* people, but they expected us to go against our beliefs and have electricity and a phone." He looked sad as he shook his head. "They wanted to buy us a car. I couldn't stay there any longer, and your aunt Missy understood. I prayed for the Lord's guidance and decided to come home.

Missy and the girls love Happiness, and Meg is thriving."

"They are happy to live in a community who readily accepts them." Jed thought of his cousins and grinned.

Arlin frowned. "Still, I worry about my girls. Who is going to keep a watchful eye on them while we're away?"

"Your sister. You know *Mam* will be there to help Aunt Missy. She may not have teenage daughters, but she has enough experience with her sons to handle any boys who come looking to spend time with my cousins."

A middle-aged woman came to their table, her arms laden with her purchases, and bought several of *Mam*'s herb and vegetable plants. Jed offered to carry them to her car. "Thank you," she said with a smile. Jed followed her to her vehicle and set the bags carefully inside before closing the trunk.

A dog barked, followed by a horn blast. He heard someone scream with alarm and then the rumble of tires spinning against gravel. Jed turned in time to see two young boys bolt out into the parking lot after a dog, into the path of an oncoming car.

"Schtupp!" he cried as, reacting quickly, he snatched the two boys, one in each arm, out of harm's way. Heart thundering in his chest, Jed set them down. He studied them carefully, noting the startled look on identical twin faces beneath their

black-banded straw hats. "Are you all right?" he asked. They nodded, and Jed released a relieved breath. "Come with me."

"Are they hurt?" Arlin asked with concern as Jed steered the boys closer to their table.

"*Nee*. Where's your *mam?*" He searched the area for their mother. The youngsters appeared too frightened by their experience to answer. Suddenly, he saw her, rushing toward them.

The young mother had bright red-gold hair beneath her white prayer *kapp*. Her eyes were the vivid blue of a clear sky on a cloudless day. She wore a dress the same blue color as her eyes with a white cape and apron. Judging by her horrified expression, Jed realized that it was her scream that he'd heard.

Sarah gave each of the twins a fierce hug before she released them. "You know better than to run out into the parking lot!" she scolded. "You could have been killed!" She grabbed each boy by the hand. "You're to stay here next to me," she stated firmly. "*Don't move*. Do you understand?" They nodded silently and cast their eyes downward. Obviously, they were too upset by the near-accident to say a word. She then took several deep calming breaths before turning a grateful gaze toward the man who'd saved them. "*Danki*," she said softly, studying the rescuer for the first time. "They escaped so fast, I didn't know where they'd gone."

"We just wanted to pet the puppy," Thomas explained and his brother nodded in agreement.

"Still, you know better than to run into the parking lot," Sarah reminded them firmly. "And to leave without permission."

"They are young boys eager to explore," the man said quietly.

"Ja," she replied, "and they are a handful on their best behavior." She closed her eyes briefly and shuddered. "I don't know what would have happened if you hadn't been nearby."

"The Lord planned for me to help." His soft answer touched a chord in her. "The boys learned a lesson and won't run into the road or parking lot without looking again...or without permission again. Will you, boys?" They looked up at their rescuer and nodded their agreement with their eyes wide.

Sarah smiled. It must be true. The Lord watched over her brothers and sent this man to help the boys when they were in trouble. She studied the man closely. "You don't live here in Delaware." The Amish man's clean-shaven face told her he was still single. "Pennsylvania," she guessed. At his nod, she asked, "Lancaster County?"

"Ja," he said. He studied her, his look making her feel warm inside. "But you live not far from here."

She blinked. "*Ja,* 'tis true…but what gave it away?"

"Your prayer *kapp.*"

Sarah smiled. "*Ja,* ours are shaped differently than the women from your area." The back of their *kapps* was round, while the women in Lancaster wore *kapps* with a back that resembled a seamed heart.

She had relatives in Pennsylvania, although it had been many years since she'd visited them. Lancaster County was home to the largest Amish population in the country. Lancaster Amish returned each week to run the shops at Spence's Bazaar Auction and Flea Market in the Farmers' Market building.

"You have a table," Sarah said.

"*Ja.* I came with my uncle to sell plants and his woodcrafts."

"Do you know anyone who runs a Farmers' Market shop?" She pointed toward a building that housed several mini shops.

"I don't know." He shrugged. "I haven't been inside the building yet."

"You should take the time to go inside," Sarah urged. "They have the best food. My cousin and I like the pork sandwiches from the meat shop." Her heart skipped a beat as cinnamon-brown eyes met hers. "This is your first time here."

"*Ja.* That is my uncle and this is our table." He gestured behind him to where an older man stood helping an *Englischer* buy a jewelry box. "Arlin made all the wooden items. I brought plants from my mother's greenhouse." He introduced his uncle as Arlin Stoltzfus.

"You both should do well here," she said after she and Arlin had greeted each other. "*Englischers* love to buy plants for their flower and vegetable gardens at Spence's." She glanced toward the man's table and spied a potato bin among the items for sale. She turned back to smile at the man. "I'll have to come back later to shop."

The man studied her with an intentness that made her nape prickle. His dark hair under his straw hat was cut in the style of Amish men. His bright brown eyes, square, firm jaw and ready smile made her tingle and glance away briefly.

Her gaze settled on his shirt. She couldn't help noticing the way his maroon broadfall shirt fit under his dark suspenders and the long length of his tri-blend denim pants legs. She had to look up to meet his gaze. He stood at least eight inches above her five-foot-one height. His arms looked firm and muscled from hard work. Sarah felt her face warm and she quickly averted her gaze.

Thomas tugged on her arm. "Can we go back to our table now?"

"We promise to be *gut* and sit nicely in the chairs," Timothy added.

Sarah studied them a moment, until she realized that they were sincere. "Go ahead. Make sure you listen to Mary Alice…and sit and behave!"

With a whoop of joy, the boys scampered back to their table. Sarah watched with relief as they kept their word and sat in their chairs. Mary Alice was busy selling baked goods. There were several people waiting in line to make a purchase. "I should get back—my cousin needs help selling our cakes and pies." She also didn't trust her brothers to behave for much longer. "*Danki* for rescuing the boys—"

He smiled. "Jedidiah Lapp."

"And I am Sarah Mast." She returned his smile. The intensity of his regard made her face heat. "I hope you sell everything you brought today, Jedidiah Lapp."

"I hope all of your cakes and pies sell quickly," he replied.

She was conscious of the man's gaze on her as she hurried back to her table. A pie, she mused. She'd bring him a cherry pie in appreciation. Perhaps purchase some plants from him for their vegetable garden.

She chanced a quick look toward his table, watching as he helped a customer make a purchase. *Jedidiah Lapp,* she thought, intrigued. He remained in her thoughts as she worked with her cousin to sell the rest of her baked goods.

As the day went on, Sarah couldn't help the occasional glance toward his table to see how Jedidiah was doing. *Normal curiosity about the man who saved my* bruders, she told herself when she caught herself looking toward him often. *Or is it?*

Later that afternoon, when she'd sold all of her baked goods but one, Sarah picked up the cherry pie she'd saved for Jedidiah and headed toward his table.

"I see you sold most of your items," Sarah said with a smile as she approached.

With an answering grin, Jedidiah came out from behind the stand. "Most, but not all. What we don't sell today, we'll sell tomorrow," he said. "Will you return?"

"Nee," Sarah said, feeling suddenly disappointed. "We had a *gut* day, too. Sold everything we intended." She handed him the pie. "I saved this for you. I hope you like cherry."

Jedidiah looked startled. "It's my favorite. How did you know?"

"I didn't," Sarah said, pleased by his reaction. "I'm glad to hear it." The man's eyes suddenly focused on something behind her. She turned and saw her young brothers as they approached.

"They don't seem too upset by the experience," Jedidiah said as he met her gaze.

"Not a bit," she agreed with a half smile. "But I can't say the same for you or me."

"When are we going for ice cream?" Thomas asked.

Timothy jerked a nod. "*Ja,* when can we go?"

"Is that any way to greet Jedidiah?" Sarah scolded.

They looked at Jedidiah and grinned. "*Hallo,* Jedidiah. Have you seen the puppy?"

"Timothy!" Sarah exclaimed, embarrassed.

The man laughed. "I'm sure my brothers and I were just like them." He tugged on the brim of the boy's hat. "Afraid I haven't seen the puppy, but don't worry—I'm sure he's all right."

Both brothers looked relieved. "We don't have a dog," Thomas said. "We want one, but *Dat* said it wouldn't be *gut* for *Mam.*"

Jedidiah studied her with a curious frown. Sarah looked away, unwilling to satisfy his curiosity. She wasn't going to tell him about her ill mother. She'd come not only to give him the pie but also to make a purchase. "I'd like four pepper and three tomato plants." She drew money from her apron pocket. "And that wooden bin."

He quickly placed the plants in a plastic bag. After the exchange of money, Jedidiah picked up the vegetable bin. "May I carry this to your buggy?"

Sarah nodded, pleased. "That would be helpful." She gestured to her brothers to follow and led

Jedidiah to her family's buggy, where Mary Alice stood outside waiting.

"Jedidiah, this is my cousin Mary Alice Troyer. Mary Alice, this is Jedidiah Lapp from Lancaster, Pennsylvania."

"Jed," Jedidiah invited, meeting Sarah's gaze with a warm smile before turning toward her cousin. "Jed is fine."

After her cousin and he greeted each other, Jedidiah leaned inside to place the bin toward the rear interior of the vehicle and straightened. "There you go."

Sarah nodded her thanks. "*Gut* sales tomorrow." She climbed into the buggy and took up the reins.

"Behave and keep out of trouble," Jedidiah said with a smile to the twins, who assured them they would try. "You should mind your *mam*."

"We will!" the boys said simultaneously.

Sarah urged the horse on and with a wave she steered the buggy out of the Spence's lot, then left onto the paved road. She glanced back once to see Jedidiah—*Jed,* she thought—still standing in the same spot. She hesitated and then waved a second time. She saw Jed lift a hand again in a silent farewell before he returned to his stand.

As she steered the horse toward home, Sarah thought of Jedidiah and sighed with regret. *Too bad I'll never get to see him again.*

Chapter Two

Saturday, after a day spent at the Sale, Jed and Arlin returned to their cousin's house and pitched in to ready the Miller property for tomorrow's church services. The bench wagon had been pulled up to the barn. Services would be held in a large open area in the new building. Jed grabbed a bench, carried it inside and set it down. "This in the right place?" he asked their cousin and host, Pete Miller.

"*Ja,* that is *gut,*" Pete said. "We'll need all of the benches in the wagon and some of the chairs from inside the house. We have guests coming from another district. I hope we have enough room."

Jedidiah studied the huge barn that had been cleared for tomorrow's use and nodded. "Looks to me like you'll seat fifty to sixty easily. Will there be more than sixty coming?"

"*Nee.*" Pete took off his straw hat and wiped his brow with his shirtsleeve. "Maybe just under fifty."

"No need to worry, then," Arlin said. "You'll have plenty of room without the chairs."

Jedidiah, Arlin and Pete made several trips with benches. Pete's two eldest sons pitched in to help finish the job, as did two other churchmen who arrived a half hour after they had. It wasn't long before the room was set up with benches on three sides facing the area where the appointed preacher would stand and speak. The women would sit on one side, the men on the other. Women with their children would remain together, listening and singing the hymns sung every church Sunday. After services, the church community would gather outside to enjoy the midday meal. The women had prepared food prior to Sunday, and cold meat, salads, vegetables and desserts would be shared among the families. The men usually ate first, with the women and children taking their meal afterward, but tomorrow would be different. The church elders had decided that families would be allowed to eat together this church Sunday.

After they'd finished with the benches and brought in the *Ausbund* hymnals, the men lingered outside and enjoyed glasses of lemonade from the pitcher that Pete's daughter Lydia had brought them. As they quenched their thirst, they chatted about Sunday services, the weather and the crops they'd planted this year.

"Pete! Arlin! You bring Jed and the others in for

supper!" Pete's wife, Mary, called out to them in the yard. She stood inside the screen door and re-directed her attention to Ned Troyer as he climbed onto the bench wagon and took up the leathers. "Ned, come inside to eat." She stepped out into the yard and approached.

"I appreciate the offer, Mary," Ned said, "but Sally is waiting for me at home." He leaned over the side of the wagon and lowered his voice. "She's made some *gut* strawberry jam." He grinned. "I convinced her to make tarts for tomorrow."

Mary smiled. "Tell her we look forward to tast-ing her tarts. The berries are extra sweet this year. I haven't made jam yet—we've been too busy eat-ing the fresh berries."

"Ja," Ned said. "Strawberry shortcake…fresh strawberries and cream. A *gut* year for Delaware strawberries!" He clicked his tongue and steered the horse toward the road. "See *ya* tomorrow."

"Ja," Pete said. He turned toward his cousins as Ned headed home. "Jed, there will be a singing here tomorrow night. I think you'll enjoy it."

Jed nodded. He enjoyed singings. Back home in Happiness, Pennsylvania, he'd been the one to lead the first hymn. He liked gathering with friends, spending time with the young people in his com-munity and those nearby. He was now older than many who attended. His brother Noah married last year. He was twenty-two and should be wed himself by now, but he hadn't found the right woman. He'd thought for a time that she might be Annie Zook, but there seemed to be something missing between them. Annie would make a wonderful wife, but she wouldn't be his. When they discussed their relationship, he and Annie had reached the conclusion that they would be better friends than sweethearts. There were other girls who watched him as if interested, but Jed didn't have strong feelings for any of them. He wanted to find a love like his brother Noah had. He longed to find a woman who fully captured his heart and loved him completely in return.

Someone is out there waiting for me. He knew it. He hoped he'd find her sooner than later. He wasn't getting any younger. He was the eldest son of Katie and Samuel Lapp, and he wondered if he'd ever find love…a love like Noah and Rachel's…a love like his *dat* and *mam*'s. He wasn't going to settle for anyone just to wed, even though he knew that many who married eventually came to love his or her spouse. It wouldn't be fair to marry any woman unless he truly loved her.

Sunday morning, Sarah sat in the back of the family buggy, a pie and a cake cradled on her lap. "You all right, *Mam?*" she asked as she leaned toward the front seat.

Her mother turned to smile at her. "*Ja,* I'm fine, Sarah. Stop your worrying."

Her *dat* glanced back briefly to meet Sarah's gaze before turning his attention toward the road. Sarah knew *Dat* was as concerned as she. It had been too long that her mother felt poorly. *Mam* was pale and constantly tired. She prayed that God would make her well soon.

"It's a lovely day for church services," Sarah said to fill the silence.

"*Ja,*" her mother agreed. "It's nice to get out and about. I look forward to visiting with our friends after church."

Sarah felt the same way. She was glad *Mam* was feeling well enough today to visit. She never missed a Sunday church service, but *Dat* usually took her home immediately afterward.

The only sound for a time was the clip-clop of their mare Jennie's hooves on the paved road as they headed toward the Millers' farm, the location for this Sunday's church services. Sarah's young twin brothers were surprisingly silent beside her. She glanced over and realized why. Just that quickly the boys had fallen asleep. Each child looked nice in his white shirt, black vest and black pants. They had managed to keep their clothes clean this morning and their usual wild mop of red hair beneath their black Sunday-best hat neatly combed. She smiled; they were miniature versions of their father. They were *gut* boys and they did listen and obey her, but still, she didn't always know what to expect from them.

There was a shift in the direction of the vehicle as Daniel Mast steered the horse onto the dirt lane that led to the Miller farm. Suddenly, *Mam* turned toward Sarah. "I don't want you to fuss over me," she said, holding her daughter's glance before shifting to send the same message silently to her husband.

"You will tell us if you're tired?" her father asked softly.

"Ja," she said. "I will come to you or send someone to find you."

"Fair enough, then," Sarah's *dat* replied as he pulled the horse into the Millers' barnyard and parked the vehicle within the row of family buggies on the left side of the dirt drive.

Dressed in his black Sunday best, Jedidiah stood on the Millers' front porch and watched as buggies rolled down the dirt lane to the farmhouse and parked in the barnyard.

"Do you know anyone?" Jed asked his uncle, who stood beside him.

"A few," Arlin said. He ran a hand over his bearded chin. "I recognize the Samuel Yoders. That's Samuel getting out of that buggy near the barn. He has five sons and a baby on the way. He lives on the neighboring farm."

"Is that his oldest son?" Jedidiah asked, studying a lad of about twelve years old.

Arlin rubbed his beard as he followed the direction of Jed's gaze. "*Ja,* that's young Abe."

Jedidiah instantly thought of his mother and wondered how she'd coped when he'd been that young age with four brothers not long behind him. It couldn't have been easy for Katie Lapp, but his *mam* had taken joy in raising her sons. It had never occurred to him how much work *Mam* had endured as a mother to five sons. And since then, she'd given birth to two more sons and a daughter.

Another vehicle pulled into the yard. Jedidiah watched casually as the driver stopped the buggy and climbed down from the carriage. The bearded older man went around to the other side to help someone out of the vehicle, while a young woman climbed from the backseat on the driver's side, a dish in each hand.

He felt his heart give a lurch, then pound rapidly as he noted the shock of red-gold hair peeking out from beneath her black bonnet. *Sarah Mast,* he thought. The young mother stood with her hands full near the buggy while her sons Thomas and Timothy scurried out after her. He saw her bend to speak briefly with the twins, watched as the boys nodded before racing toward a group of youngsters who stood waiting outside the barn for church services. He saw the driver—Sarah's husband? *Nee,* her *dat,* he suspected—had helped someone out of the carriage. *Sarah's mother?*

Jed frowned. *Where is Sarah's husband?*

He watched Sarah pause to wait for the other woman to catch up before they headed toward the Miller farmhouse together. The older woman carried a basket. Jedidiah didn't know what possessed him to move in her direction, but within seconds, he was reaching out to relieve the frail older woman of her burden. "Let me," he said with a smile. The basket wasn't heavy.

Sarah's mother looked up at him and responded in kind. "'Tis nice of you," the woman gasped, out of breath.

Jed turned toward her daughter. "Sarah," he greeted. "I didn't expect to see you here."

"Jedidiah." Sarah looked surprised to see him. Her voice was soft and slightly breathless. "I thought you would have gone home by now."

"Nee. We leave tomorrow." He could sense Sarah's *mam*'s curiosity. He nodded at the woman respectfully.

Sarah made introductions. "*Mam,* this is Jedidiah—" She paused a second. "Jed—"

"Lapp," he supplied, amused.

"Ja." Sarah nodded and Jed saw her blush as she looked away. "We met at the Sale. He's from Lancaster. Jed was the man I told you about—the one who grabbed the twins before they got hit by

a car." She turned to Jed. "Jed, this is Ruth Mast, my *mam*."

Jed took off his hat. "Nice to meet you."

Her mother stopped to study him more closely, making Jed slightly uncomfortable under the intensity of her regard. And then the woman smiled, and Jed relaxed. "Thank the Lord that you were there to save my sons," she said. Unlike Sarah's red-gold hair, Ruth's hair was dark brown with streaks of soft gray. Sarah had inherited her mother's features—nose, chin, smile, but not her hair or eye color. Ruth's eyes were green, while Sarah's gaze was a vivid shade of bright blue.

Jed glanced over to check on Ruth's progress. Satisfied that she was managing, he held out a hand for Sarah's cake plate. With Ruth's basket in one arm and Sarah's cake plate in the other, he escorted the two women to the Miller house. Mary Miller came to the door as they climbed the porch steps.

"Ruth! Sarah!" Mary greeted as she came forward to accept the family's food offerings.

"Ruth's," Jed explained as he handed his cousin the basket and gave Edna Byler, a neighbor who'd followed closely behind Mary, Sarah's cake. "I will talk with you later," he told the two women.

"Will you sit at our table for the midday meal?" Ruth asked.

Jed smiled. "I would like that."

"We will see you then," Sarah's mother said as she carefully climbed the porch steps.

Sarah nodded as Jed met her gaze before she followed her mother into the house. Jed looked back to see her standing at the screen door. She quickly moved inside and disappeared from sight.

Sons? He suddenly realized what Ruth had said. *Thank the Lord that you were there to save my sons.* The twins weren't Ruth's grandsons, nor were they Sarah's sons, Jed realized. They were Ruth's sons…and Sarah's brothers!

And now he understood why there was no husband in sight for Sarah. She wasn't married and didn't have children! Jed suddenly felt elated.

I'll be eating at Sarah's table. Jed was pleased at Ruth's invitation. He was leaving tomorrow, but until then, he could enjoy the day, learning more about Sarah Mast. He grinned happily, buoyed by the prospect.

Soon, the community and their guests gathered for church inside the Millers' new barn. The service began with a hymn from the *Ausbund.* Jed realized that his community back in Happiness, Pennsylvania, sang the same hymn during services, but the melody was different. Still, Jed was able to catch on quickly, and he sang the hymn with confidence with the rest of the congregation.

Jed saw Sarah, who was seated beside her mother and twin brothers, listen intently as Preacher Byler addressed the church members. He couldn't help look her way from time to time until he saw her glance in his direction and then back over her shoulder as if she could tell someone was watching her.

He focused his full attention on the preacher and didn't gaze in Sarah's direction again...although he was conscious of her for the rest of the service.

Sarah tried not to look in Jedidiah's direction, but a prickling along the back of her neck made her wonder if he'd been watching her. Several times she glanced his way only to see that he paid strict attention to Sunday services. Sarah realized that she must have imagined his stare. But then the feeling of being watched came back so strongly that she took a quick look behind her. If Jed wasn't studying her, then who was?

Jed stood outside the barn door as Sarah left with her twin brothers. "May I help carry out the food?" he asked.

Sarah shook her head. "We can manage. You'd best join the men. There's my *dat*. You can sit at that table. The rest of us will join you shortly." She watched as her two older brothers sat down near her father. "There is Toby and Ervin. They are older than me."

Jed studied the two young men who sat across from their father. "How many siblings do you have?"

"Besides the twins and the two eldest?" she

asked. He nodded. "I have an older sister. Emma married and moved to Ohio with her husband, James."

"I see." Jed seemed thoughtful as he looked away briefly. "Then you are the only daughter at home." He focused his eyes on her.

"Ja," Sarah admitted. Jed's intense regard made her quickly look away.

"Your *mam*...she is unwell?"

Taken off guard, Sarah flashed him a look. "She says she is fine."

"But you don't believe it." His voice was soft.

Sarah sighed as she felt the warmth of his concern. *"Nee.* She has been tired and sick for weeks now."

His expression filled with sympathy. "Is there anything I can do?"

His response surprised her. "I appreciate your kindness. *Ja,* there is something you can do...pray for her."

"I shall keep her in my prayers," Jed said quietly.

Sarah blinked back tears. *"Danki."* She took a deep breath and pulled herself together. "I must go inside. Please...feel free to sit at our family table. I can introduce you first if you'd like."

Jed suddenly grinned, and Sarah felt her face warm. "Go help inside. I can introduce myself." He turned and headed toward the table.

Sarah stood a moment as she saw Jed speak with

her father and brothers, watched as her father gestured for Jed to sit across from him. Her brothers
shifted on the bench to make room for Jed, who
then sat next to her eldest brother, Ervin. Relieved
at how well her family appeared to receive him,
Sarah headed toward the Miller farmhouse.

Sarah felt a lurch in her chest as she entered the
house with thoughts of Jedidiah. Women filled
Mary's kitchen, working to unwrap food that had
been prepared previously. She attempted to force
Jed from her mind. "What can I do to help?" she
asked as Mary set a casserole dish on the counter.

"You can start with those," her mother said, gesturing toward platters of meat and bowls of salads.
She uncovered a bowl of potato salad and moved
to place it next to the casserole dish.

Mary gestured for her mother to sit. "Ruth Mast,
don't you overdo!" She smiled at Sarah's mother.
"We like having you here."

Sarah was happy to see her mother take a seat.
"I'll be careful," *Mam* said.

Pleased that her mother was able to join the day's
meal, Sarah made numerous trips outside as she
carried platters of cold meat, bowls of homemade
potato salad and coleslaw, and dried corn casserole
to the food tables. She was glad that Mary refused
to let her mother carry anything, happier yet to note
that Ruth Mast didn't object but remained seated in
the kitchen until all of the food had been uncovered

or unearthed from the gas refrigerator and brought outside. After the meal, they would take the leftovers inside and return to put out the desserts.

Men, women and children mingled, enjoying the food. Sarah set down the last dish on the food table. Where was Jed? She didn't immediately see him at her family table. She searched the grounds until she found him standing by a tree not far from the table as if he was waiting for her. His eyes brightened as Jed watched her approach. He nodded as she drew closer.

"Hungry?" he asked.

Sarah inclined her head. "You?" His answer was a slow smile that did odd things to her insides.

The food was set up as a buffet for folks to fill their plates. *Should I ask him what he wants to eat?* she wondered. She needed to fix a plate for *Mam*. Then her thoughts centered on the brush of his hand on her arm, the touch of his arm against hers, as they walked side by side toward the buffet tables. Sarah felt her heart pumping hard and she had trouble concentrating as she followed behind Jed and they each filled plates. She was puzzled at first when she saw Jed fix a second plate, asking her opinion as he chose food. It was then that she realized that he was filling a plate for her mother. Touched by his thoughtfulness, she blinked back tears.

They went back to the table to find two seats

vacant across from each other. When Jed set the plate before *Mam,* then took his seat, Sarah's mother seemed as moved by Jed's kindness as Sarah had been.

Sarah enjoyed the cold roast beef, dried-corn casserole and potato salad, while Jed, she noted, had chosen a slice of ham, sweetened green beans and a huge helping of macaroni salad. They looked at each other's plates, saw the differences and chuckled.

"I like it all," Jed said.

Sarah nodded, but she realized that he had chosen carefully for her mother. "I love those beans, but I get them whenever I want, since I made them using *Mam*'s recipe."

Jed's eyes flickered. "You bake *and* cook."

Sarah nodded. "*Ja,* of course." She didn't want to tell him that she'd been doing all of the cooking these past few months, that *Mam* was too tired and feeling poorly to do much more than peel potatoes or snap the ends off store-bought fresh green beans. She saw that he'd guessed the truth by the way he studied her.

Everyone enjoyed the meal. Sarah was pleased to see how at ease Jed seemed in the company of her family, and she smiled and laughed as her father told stories of her twin brothers' antics on their farm. For Sarah, the meal passed too quickly.

Chapter Three

"I'll be going home tomorrow," Jedidiah said to her family as they lingered over the remainder of their meal. "Arlin and I came to Spence's Bazaar—the Sale, you call it?" Sarah nodded. "We had many things to sell—and we sold everything we had. My uncle is eager to head back to his family. He has five daughters, and he worries about them."

Sarah silently wished he could stay longer.

"I understand that Arlin made Ruth's new vegetable bin," Daniel Mast said.

Jed paused in the act of eating potato salad. "*Ja*. Arlin works well with wood. Just like my *vadder* and my brother Noah."

"How many brothers and sisters do you have?" her mother inquired.

"Six brothers and a little sister. My *mam* keeps busy but she enjoys all of us. *Mam* grew the vegetable plants Sarah purchased in her greenhouse."

Sarah checked her mother's reaction. She smiled as if she enjoyed hearing about Jed's life in Pennsylvania. Sarah didn't like the thought of him leaving.

"There is Arlin by the barn talking with Ned Troyer." Jed flashed her a grin, and Sarah blushed.

"I'd better help bring out the desserts." She stood and resisted the urge to straighten her bonnet.

"I'm eager for a slice of your pie, Sarah," her *dat* said.

"Me, too." Jed's soft voice vibrated down her spine.

Sarah hesitated when Arlin stopped by to chat. Jed introduced Arlin to her family. "*Mam* likes the vegetable bin I bought for her," she told Jed's uncle with a smile. "Hers needed replacing, and yours is well made."

Arlin looked pleased. "I hope it gives you many year's of *gut* use."

"I'm sure it will," *Mam* said.

Soon, Arlin left to rejoin his cousin Pete at another table, and Sarah grabbed leftovers from the food table to carry inside. After the desserts were put out, she returned to her family…and Jed.

"Dessert!" Timothy exclaimed, climbing over the bench and running toward the food. Thomas jumped up and raced after him, eager to get there first.

Ervin stood and straddled the bench, watching

his young brothers choose sweets from the dessert table. "*Mam, Dat,* want anything in particular?"

"I'd like to try one of Sally Troyer's strawberry tarts," her *mam* said.

Sarah started to rise. "I'll get it."

She shook her head. "Sit. Your brother will get it for me." She flashed Ervin a smile.

Ervin rose and Toby followed. "I'm thinking of chocolate cake," Toby said, and his older brother grinned.

Feeling Jed's gaze, Sarah shifted uncomfortably on the bench. "*Mam,* can I get you some lemonade?" She wasn't used to sitting. It made her feel guilty when she knew how much her *mam* needed her.

Timothy and Thomas returned to the table, each carrying plates that threatened to tip and spill. "Jedidiah!" they cried in unison, "we got cake!"

"Looks good!" Teasingly, Jed reached out as if to grab Thomas's plate. "What is that? Carrot cake?" he asked.

Thomas nodded and cradled his plate protectively. "It tastes good. Want me to get you some?"

"It looks delicious, but I'll go over and get some myself—when your sister Sarah is ready for dessert."

The boys turned to Sarah. "There are lots of cakes and pies, Sissy," Timothy said.

Hearing her name on Jed's lips infused her with pleasure. "I'm thinking about chocolate-cream pie," she said. She could feel Jed's regard, and although feeling a bit shaky, she managed to smile at him. "I'm ready for dessert. Shall we go?" She stood and smoothed out her apron.

Jed grinned and rose. "Chocolate-cream pie?" he asked as they headed toward the dessert table.

"Maybe," Sarah said with amusement, "or maybe not. I won't know what I want until I see it."

He chuckled. "I'm thinking I'll have more than one thing."

"I may, too," she replied with a sudden feeling of gladness. The day was bright and sunny, and life was good.

The lingering memory of Jed's answering laughter did strange things to her insides as Sarah selected a slice of chocolate-cream pie and a piece of peanut-butter fudge.

Jed, she saw, chose peach cobbler and a piece of her cherry pie. *His favorite kind of pie,* she remembered, pleased.

Sarah enjoyed spending the day in Jed's company. She liked seeing him with her family. She knew her parents well enough to know when they liked someone, and they liked Jedidiah. It was too bad that he lived in Pennsylvania. She reminded herself that this was simply a day to remember. Tomorrow Jed would leave and Sarah would never see him again. It was just as well, since she needed to be near for *Mam.*

Soon it was afternoon and the women had begun to clean the tables and collect the leftovers. Sarah rose. "Time to help Mary in the kitchen." And it was time to check on her mother, who had gone inside moments earlier.

"I enjoyed spending time with your family," Jed said, his brown eyes glowing.

Sarah averted her glance from the warmth in his gaze. "It was a nice day."

"Sarah!" *Mam* stood at the screen door. "Would you please bring in the rest of the desserts?"

She smiled in her mother's direction. *"Ja, Mam."*

"Please see me before you leave," Jed said. "There is something I'd like to talk with you about."

Warmth curled in her belly as she nodded. "Is everything all right?"

"Ja, of course. I want to talk with you about the singing here this evening."

A singing, she thought. It had been a long time since she'd attended a singing. But thoughts of her mother's health tamped down her joy. How could she leave *Mam?* She heard Jed talking with her older brothers as she headed toward the house. Wouldn't it be nice to spend a few more hours with him before he left for home?

Later, after the women had cleaned up after the meal and put away the food, Sarah came out of the Miller house and spied Jed seated in a chair on the front porch.

He stood when he saw her. "I spoke with your brothers. They are attending the singing tonight. Will you come?"

"I don't know if I can.... *Mam*..."

Jed nodded as if he understood.

"I'd like to come," she was quick to add. "I'll be sorry to see the day end." Then she glanced away as she wondered how he might have interpreted her words.

"The day is not over," he said softly. "Your mother seems well today."

"*Ja,* 'tis true." Sarah wanted nothing more than to stay. "I'll check with *Mam* to see if she needs me."

"Your brothers will be there," he told her. His voice dropped. "I'd like to take you home afterward."

Sarah's heart started to race. Wouldn't it be exciting to go to the singing and be driven home by Jedidiah Lapp! "I'll check," she said and fled back into the house to ask her mother. Her heart beat wildly as she entered the kitchen and searched for *Mam*. It had been a long time since she'd gone to a singing. For months now, concern for her *mam* had kept her home.

But *Mam* had done surprisingly well this day. Was it possible that her mother would be fine and that she could attend?

She caught sight of her mother seated in a chair in the Millers' great room. "*Mam*." She approached, almost afraid to ask; she didn't want to be disappointed. "There is a singing tonight—"

"Ja!" Mary Miller said. "It will be *gut* for you to go."

Sarah didn't want to miss it, but she wouldn't put her wishes above her mother's needs.

"Sarah," her *mam* said with a smile, "you should stay." She frowned as if it had just occurred to her how much her youngest daughter had missed during these past months. "It's been a long time for you."

"It's all right," Sarah assured her. "I'll come home with you and *Dat,* but if you are feeling well enough, I'd like to return. Ervin and Toby are going. I can ride back with them."

"Or you could stay and one of my sons can take you home," Mary Miller said. "I'm sure P.J. would be happy to see you home."

"I'd be happy to bring her home," Jed said as he stepped into the room.

Sarah felt his presence immediately. It vibrated in the room, making her fully aware of him. She watched her mother study the young man and nod. "As long as you get home safely," Ruth directed toward her daughter. "Where is your *dat?*" She stood, wobbling a little on unsteady legs before righting herself.

"Daniel is outside near the barn with Pete, Arlin and Ned Troyer," Jedidiah offered. Someone called him from outside. "Arlin," he explained with a smile before he left to return to the men who were gathered out in the yard. Sarah felt the loss of his presence.

"And what of the twins?" her mother asked. As if exhausted, she sat down again. "Have you seen them?"

"They are outside with my two youngest." Sally Troyer reached back to retie her apron strings. "They are getting along just fine. Perhaps your boys would like to spend the night with my Joseph and John."

Her heart gave a little lurch. Without the twins to wreak havoc on the house, Sarah could attend the singing, leaving her mother to rest quietly with her *dat* nearby.

"I think Timothy and Thomas would like that," *Mam* said. She focused her gaze on Sarah. "You'd like to go?"

Sarah nodded. "*Ja,* but I can stay home if you need me."

"*Nee,*" she said, "there is no reason for you to stay. I will be fine. Now, where did you say Daniel is?" Her eyes lit up as she spied her husband out the window. "Ah, there he is!"

"I'll tell him we are ready to go," Sarah said with quiet joy.

Mam frowned. "I thought you'd stay."

Sarah shook her head. "I will see you settled before I return with Ervin and Toby."

Her *mam*'s expression grew soft. "You are a *gut* daughter." She stood a bit wobbly but managed to right herself without help. "I will come with you to get your *vadder*."

"I can bring back clean clothes for the twins," Sarah offered as she helped her mother across the room.

"No need," Sally assured her. "They will be fine." She grinned, apparently pleased with the turn of events. "I'll tell them they'll be staying with us tonight."

Sarah could hear her young brothers' whoops of happiness as she and her mother joined her father outside. "Sounds like they are excited to be spending the night with the Troyers."

Daniel grinned. "It will be a nice quiet evening for us," he said.

Her mother's smile was weak but genuine. "I did well today," she declared. With help, she climbed into the buggy and sat down.

"Ja, Mam." Sarah set a blanket about her mother's legs. "Time to go home and rest."

Once *Mam* was situated comfortably, Sarah climbed into the back and then gazed out the window as *Dat* pulled the buggy away from the farmhouse down the dirt lane toward the main road. She thought she'd caught a glimpse of Jed watching them as they drove away.

This evening, she would be spending more time

with Jedidiah Lapp. Heart thumping, she thought of the evening ahead with barely controlled excitement.

Jed stood on the Millers' front porch and watched as buggies and wagons arrived with young people who had come for the evening's singing. There was still no sign of either Sarah or her brothers. Would she come or did her mother need her?

Why should I care if she stays home? It wasn't as if he'd ever see her again. Still, the memory of her smiling face and blue eyes lingered in his thoughts. He had enjoyed his time with her family. The afternoon had passed quickly—too quickly.

He shouldn't think of Sarah. He was too old for her. What was she? Seventeen? Eighteen? He'd thought he'd found someone he might love in Annie Zook, but he'd been wrong. If he'd hurt her, Annie hadn't shown it. Sarah was vulnerable. She'd spent a long time caring for her mother. She hadn't been to a singing in months. He had no right to monopolize her time, but he couldn't help himself.

If she comes, then I'll enjoy the evening with her and then say goodbye. She would find someone else here in Delaware to love. She would want to stay near her family, and he needed to be home in Happiness.

It was growing late and still there was no sign of

any of the Masts. Jed stepped down from the porch and crossed the yard, more than mildly disappointed.

Suddenly, a buggy came barreling down the dirt drive to pull up quickly behind the line of vehicles. Jed saw Ervin and Toby jump down from the vehicle, but no sign of Sarah. He waited for the brothers to join him before entering the barn.

Just as he had given up hope of seeing her again, Jed watched Sarah climb out carefully after her brothers, balancing a plate in one hand. Ervin helped his sister, grabbing the plate from her hand. The siblings turned and spied Jed standing in the yard. Ervin waved, and Toby followed his eldest brother, while Sarah came slowly behind.

Jed felt a sudden lightening of spirit. Sarah was here, and he would get to spend more time with her, if only for a few hours.

He grinned at Sarah's brothers, and then he waited with a soft smile as Sarah caught up to them. "Nice night for a singing," he said, noting her flushed cheeks and sparkling eyes.

"Ja," she said. "It's been a long time since I've had the joy." She gestured toward the plate Ervin held out to her. "I brought cookies—chocolate chip."

"This will be a *gut* night, Sarah," he whispered as the brothers went into the barn ahead of them.

She gave a barely perceptible nod as they followed. Then, there were greetings from the others who had come. Jed noticed that his cousin P.J. seemed particularly happy to see Sarah. P.J., Pete's eldest son, was closer in age to Sarah than he. He tried not to be upset by the fact that once he left, it could be P.J. who would eventually keep company with Sarah and perhaps win her heart.

Don't let it bother you tonight, he thought. They had this one night together, and he planned to enjoy every single moment of it.

Chapter Four

Sarah felt gladdened by the greetings of her friends and neighbors as she entered the barn and took a seat across from Jedidiah. She was conscious of Jed's presence as she smiled and returned Miriam Yost's wave. She hadn't seen Miriam in a long time. She liked the young woman. Sarah suddenly realized how much she'd missed socializing with her friends since her mother had become ill.

"Sarah," Pete and Mary Miller's oldest son, P.J., greeted her. "It is *gut* to have you with us again."

She smiled at him. "It is nice to be here." She sensed Jed watching her, and she flashed him a glance.

His eyes warmed as their gazes met. He smiled, and Sarah felt her breath catch. His attention was focused on her, and she felt the touch of his brown gaze as if he'd brushed her arm or captured her hand with his fingers.

But there was nothing untoward in his regard of her, she realized. The thoughts—the feelings—were all hers, and she pulled herself together, prepared to enjoy the events of the night's singing.

To her surprise, P.J., also known as Pete Jr., began the singing with his choice of hymn from the *Ausbund.* He sang the first verse before everyone joined in. As Jed joined in, Sarah heard his pleasant, vibrant tone. She was pleased when he began the second hymn, the *Loblied,* his voice rising in praise of the Lord. She could feel his conviction, his passion for God, and Sarah knew that her thoughts of him were accurate. He was a *gut* man with a kind heart and true love for the Lord. She sang out happily, her voice rising with the others as they finished the hymn they had all sung that morning during church services.

After a third hymn, Miriam Yost's brother Joseph suggested they stop for some refreshment.

"You are always wanting to eat," his sister teased.

Joseph shrugged. "We can sing another hymn, if you'd prefer."

"I could use one of Sarah's cookies," Jed said.

Sarah flushed as everyone turned to look at her. Jed's smile put her at ease, and she sent him a silent message of thanks.

As it was, the majority decided light refreshments were in order before they continued with hymns and games.

Lydia Miller, Mary and Pete's only daughter, had made lemonade and iced tea for all to enjoy. Sarah helped Lydia to distribute drinks, before she grabbed her plate of cookies and a platter of lemon bars that Miriam Yost had made for the occasion.

Jed, Sarah noticed, was quick to choose one of her cookies. He took a bite and flashed her an appreciative smile. Everyone had left their seat to mingle in the open area of the large barn.

Jed took another bite of the cookie. "You will let me take you home tonight, won't you?" he asked.

"My brothers are here—"

Jed gestured toward where Ervin was deep in conversation with Elizabeth Yoder. Not far from Ervin, Toby chatted with Elizabeth's older sister Alice. "I think Ervin and Toby have plans to take those two home. Wouldn't you rather ride with me?"

Sarah hesitated. She knew she'd rather have Jedidiah take her home, but she didn't know if she should go with him. Yet, how would she feel riding along with her brothers and the Yoder sisters?

"I will ride home with you," she said quietly so that no one but Jed would hear.

Jed grinned. "*Gut!* I will look forward to taking you," he said as the others began to head back to their seats.

Sarah was conscious that Jed allowed her to precede him, and as she sat down, she tried not to look at him, but she couldn't help herself.

She found him studying her with an intensity that made her feel odd inside. She couldn't say that she disliked the feeling. Being the focus of this kind man's attention was not unwelcome. *He leaves tomorrow,* she reminded herself. *I will never see him again.*

Will he write? she wondered. She wasn't going to ask him; it wouldn't be right unless he mentioned it first.

As her friend Miriam chose and began the next hymn, Sarah decided to forget tomorrow and simply enjoy the evening…and the ride home with Jedidiah Lapp. Riding home with a young man from a singing was a rare treat, and she savored the thought of it.

The singing flew by quickly, filled with song and games, and delicious food.

Sarah went to search for her brothers afterward to tell them that Jed would be taking her home. There was an awkward moment when P.J. Miller offered to bring her home. Sarah had to tell him that she already had a ride.

"Jedidiah is taking me," she said. She felt badly when she saw the young man's face fall. "Maybe another time?"

His quick look of gladness made her slightly uncomfortable. She shouldn't have said anything, but she hadn't wanted him to feel bad.

"Jed will bring me home tonight," she told Ervin.

Ervin didn't seem surprised. "That's nice, Sissy. We will be home as soon as we can." He glanced over to where Toby and the two Yoder sisters stood. "We will be making a stop on the way."

Sarah nodded, then teased, "Do not take the long way to the Yoder farm, Ervin Mast."

Ervin looked stunned at first by her teasing, but then he grinned, obviously pleased. "We don't appreciate you enough…what you do for *Mam*."

"I am the daughter, and I love *Mam*. Emma isn't here, so it is up to me."

Ervin leaned closer to whisper in Sarah's ear, "You must take time to enjoy your life, Sarah. I know your hard work is not merely a duty to you, but an expression of love. I will try to help more."

Sarah's eyes filled with tears. "I don't know what to say."

Ervin grinned. "There is Jed. He's brought the wagon around, and he is waiting for you. Keep your words for your ride home."

As she headed toward the wagon by which Jedidiah stood patiently waiting for her with his hat in his hands, Sarah thought of her brother's words and wondered what he meant by taking the time to enjoy her life more. She prayed to the Lord and did what she could to live life the way He would want it. She couldn't take time away from *Mam,* not until it was certain that she was well again.

* * *

Jed studied her expression as Sarah approached. She seemed upset. Why? He had seen her talking with his cousin P.J. Would she rather he was taking her home? His concern vanished as Sarah offered him a genuine smile as she reached him. He lifted his black felt hat, then set it back onto his head.

"*Ja.* I let Ervin know that I would not be riding home with him."

"And did he mind?" he asked.

The corners of her blue eyes crinkled. "*Nee.* As you suspected, my brothers will not be going directly home. They have plans that include stopping by the Yoder farm."

"And so you are stuck with me."

"*Nee,* I am not stuck, Jedidiah Lapp."

Her answer delighted him, and he studied her fondly. "*Gut,*" he said as his spirits rose with the prospect of spending a little more time with her. He would like the memory of the evening to take home to Happiness with him. He would like to see her farm, to picture her out in the yard or in the farmhouse, going about her chores, caring for the twins and her family.

He held out his hand, and Sarah looked at it a moment before their fingers touched as she accepted his help onto the wagon seat.

The night was a typical late-spring evening. The temperature was cool, but not cold. There was a full moon, which lit up the dark sky and shed a beam of brightness onto the yard. Jed felt sorry to release her hand as he climbed up onto the wagon seat beside her.

"All set?" he asked, and she nodded. "Are you cold?" She shook her head. "Are you going to be silent during the entire ride?"

"Nee," she said with what sounded like horror.

He laughed. "I am teasing you, Sarah Mast." Then with a click of his tongue and a flick of the leathers, he steered the horse down the long dirt lane and then turned right onto the main road. He glanced at Sarah and saw her look back as if seeking her brothers. "They will linger awhile before they leave," he said.

She nodded. "I didn't know that both of them are sweet on the Yoder sisters."

Jed shrugged. "Why would any sister know? Unless she can read her brothers' thoughts."

"Praise the Lord that I can't," Sarah said with such feeling that Jed laughed out loud.

He saw her lips curve before her laughter joined his.

"Shall we take the long way home?" he asked, expecting her to decline.

To his surprise, she said, "You are the driver." She frowned. "Do you know where I live?"

"Ja, I asked directions and realized that Arlin and I drove by on our way back from the Sale."

She seemed content with his answer, and he drove at the slowest pace he could manage with the horse. He wouldn't take the long way home; it wouldn't be fair to her when he was leaving tomorrow. He would enjoy this time with her, even if in silence. Having her on the seat next to him was enough to keep him happy.

He didn't like the thought of leaving her, of never seeing her again, but what could he do? They both had responsibilities and family in two communities a long distance from each other. If only she lived in Lancaster, or his family resided here in Kent County, Delaware.

But the Lord had granted him the pleasure of knowing her if only for a brief time, and he would pray to the Lord to help him when he was home again…to get on with his life…and find a woman to love and become his bride.

All too soon for Sarah, Jed was steering the wagon onto the driveway that led to her family farmhouse.

They had chatted easily, sharing stories of their siblings. As time passed and the Mast farm drew nearer, silence had reigned between them. Sarah wanted to say something, admit how much she'd enjoyed his company, but she was reluctant to do so. He knew her situation. Perhaps he was just being kind.

She was conscious of the sound of the wagon

wheels over dirt and gravel as Jed steered closer to her house.

Soon, too soon, Sarah thought, the wagon was in her yard, at her front door.

Jed jumped down and rounded the vehicle to help her. He didn't extend his hand as he had before. He simply reached up and grabbed her waist. She blushed, feeling the heat in her neck and cheeks, the tingling of his hands on her waist, as he promptly released her and stepped back. The action took only seconds, but Sarah knew she'd remember the moment for a lifetime.

"Home," he announced. It was the first time Sarah thought that he looked uncomfortable.

"I appreciate the ride," she offered shyly. "I hope God grants you a safe journey home tomorrow."

He hesitated a few seconds. "I will remember this night, Sarah Mast."

"As will I," she admitted, her heart beating wildly.

Neither spoke as they looked out into the yard as if studying the way the moonlight played on the barn and property. Sarah chanced a look at Jed. His handsome features were clearly visible under the bright moonbeam. She saw that he looked troubled.

"Is anything wrong?" she asked, knowing that she shouldn't ask.

Jed turned, then smiled, and suddenly it was as if she had only imagined his sadness.

The sound of a buggy coming down the dirt lane toward the house heralded the arrival of her brothers. She didn't want her last moments with Jed to be witnessed by her older siblings.

"Jed…" she began.

"I will miss you, Sarah," he said.

She blinked back tears. "And I will miss you." She bit her lip. "I had fun today and this evening. I will thank the Lord for the moment when you stepped in to save my brothers."

His smile was warm. "Did you know I first thought you were their mother?"

She looked stunned. "You did?"

"*Ja.* And I was disappointed, for I knew you must be wed."

Her brothers' buggy pulled into the barnyard. He glanced their way and seemed to feel the same urgency that she did. "I am glad you weren't wed or I would not have had this time with you." He grew quiet and then said, "I regret that the Lapp family farm is not in Kent County, Delaware."

Ervin and Toby had climbed out of their wagon and approached them.

"Farewell, Sarah Mast," Jed said, sending her a look that she would never forget.

"Farewell and safe journey, Jedidiah Lapp. Give my regards to Arlin."

He nodded and then spoke briefly to her brothers

before he climbed back onto the wagon and turned the horse for the Miller home.

Sarah stood, watching as the wagon headed down the lane, overwhelmed by a bittersweet mixture of sadness and pleasure.

Ervin came to stand next to her. "You like him."

"Ja."

"He lives far from Delaware."

"I know," she whispered, then managed to grin at her brother. "I don't know about you, but I'm ready for bed."

Ervin studied her a moment and seemed satisfied by what he saw. "I could use something to eat."

Sarah laughed. "What?"

"Pie?"

"There may be a slice of apple or chocolate cream left."

Ervin grinned. "Singing makes me hungry," he said as they headed into the house.

Toby had already gone inside. Apparently, the singing had made him hungry as well, for he was already in the kitchen, delving into the extra cookies she'd made yesterday afternoon.

Later that night, as she lay in bed unable to sleep, Sarah thought of Jedidiah Lapp and the time she'd spent with him. As she chose to remember the warmth of his cinnamon-brown eyes and quick, ready smile instead of the fact that tomorrow he would be gone, Sarah finally fell asleep with a pleased smile on her face.

But when she woke the next morning, she thought of him leaving…then she tried not to think of him any more as she went about her daily chores and checked to see if her mother needed anything.

Still, she couldn't get him out of her mind.

Chapter Five

Jedidiah Lapp had left Kent County a month ago,
yet Sarah couldn't stop thinking about him. She
recalled the warmth in his brown gaze, the dark
brown hair beneath his wide-brimmed banded
hat, his grin. She knew she should forget him, but
spending time with him had been a wonderful experience. She had enjoyed his company, his smile…
the way he'd made her laugh…his pleasant voice
lifted in song when they'd attended the singing that
evening. She and Jed had talked during the buggy
ride home. She had loved every second she'd spent
with him.

It was late morning and Sarah was upstairs making the beds in the twins' room. The sun shone
brightly through the window and streamed golden
against the sheets as she tucked them beneath
the mattress. She picked up Thomas's blue shirt
and hung it on a wall hook near his bed. Spying

a straw hat, she bent to retrieve it. As she set the hat on Timothy's bed, she thought of her parents. *Mam* and *Dat* were sleeping downstairs now. Her mother's strength was weakening, and Sarah knew she'd have to discuss her health with *Dat* soon.

"Sarah!" Her older brother Tobias stood at the bottom of the stairs as Sarah came out of the twins' bedroom to the top landing. Toby had been working on the farm. He'd pushed back his straw hat and there was a streak of dirt across his forehead and on his left cheek.

"*Ja,* Toby?" Sarah descended the stairs.

Toby tugged on his suspenders. "*Mam* needs you." He readjusted his hat, pulling the brim low.

Sarah hurried down the rest of the steps. "Is she all right?"

Her brother shrugged. "Seems to be. Except for being tired all the time."

Sarah sighed as she left him, shaking her head as she crossed the family gathering area toward the small room where her parents now slept. At times she didn't know what to make of her older brother. Didn't Tobias realize their mother was ill? Their eldest brother, Ervin, understood the situation better than she'd expected, certainly better than Tobias did. Lately, she'd caught Ervin watching their *mudder* with an intentness that was telling. Last evening, he had discussed his concerns with her, and she'd been surprised that Ervin was worried about her as much as he was for *Mam*.

"Mam?" Sarah entered the bedroom, saw Ruth seated in a chair by the window. "Are you all right?"

She turned toward her with barely a smile and gestured for Sarah to sit on the bed. "Come in, Sarah. I need to talk with you."

Sarah felt her insides lurch as she nodded and sat on the patchwork quilt. "Is it about your recent doctor's visit?"

"Ja." Ruth turned to fully face her daughter and reached to clasp Sarah's hands. "There is something I need to tell you." The daylight emphasized the tired lines in *Mam*'s face. She looked exhausted and much older than her forty-three years. "I need heart surgery. The doctor believes he can fix it, but it will take me a while to recover."

"Surgery?" Sarah breathed. She could feel the weakness in her mother's grip. She fought to stifle her fear, to keep her thoughts hidden. "That is something," she murmured, "and I'll be here to help."

"Nee," Ruth said. "We're sending you with the twins to our cousins William and Josie in Pennsylvania."

"But *Mam*—what if you need me?" Send her away? No, she didn't want to go. How could she leave *Mam?* "Can't I stay?"

"Nee. It's best if you take the boys. I love Timothy

and Thomas dearly, but they are a handful. Josie has boys near the same age. Your brothers will enjoy staying with them. I need you to go to make sure they behave."

"What about Emma?" she asked. "Can't she take the boys?" Her older sister was married but had no children. If Emma took the twins, Sarah could stay behind to care for *Mam*.

Her mother rubbed the back of her neck as if it pained her. Catching Sarah's concerned look, she smiled weakly and dropped her hand. "Your sister hasn't been married a full year. I don't want her to worry about your brothers. Soon, she'll have a brood of her own. And Ohio is too far. I want you and the boys nearby, in case…"

"*Nee, Mam!* The Lord will heal you. We just have to pray." Sarah felt a weight settle in her stomach at the thought that her mother might not fight to get better. "You'll have the surgery, and you *will* get well. I'll do as you say and take the twins to William and Josie's until you call for us to come home." She bit her lip. "But you must have faith."

Her mother reached out to touch Sarah's cheek. "You are a *gut* and kind daughter, Sarah."

Tears filled Sarah's eyes as she reached up to cover her mother's hand, pressing it lightly against her cheek. "I wish I could stay," she whispered.

"I know you do," *Mam* said. "But your *dat* and

I have discussed this, and we believe this is for the best."

Dat felt the same way? Sarah sighed inwardly as she resigned herself to the trip. She was a dutiful daughter; she wouldn't argue with her parents. "When do we leave?"

"The day after tomorrow. We've hired Mr. Colter to drive you."

Mr. Colter was their neighbor and an *Englischer*.

"So soon?" Sarah's spirits plummeted when her mother nodded. "We'll be ready," she assured her. "I'd better see that the twins' clothes are laundered for the trip." Sarah had to swallow against a painful lump as she rose to her feet. She bent to hug her mother. "I love you, *Mam*."

She gave her a genuine smile. "I love you, Sarah."

Lancaster County, Pennsylvania

Jedidiah pulled the family buggy to the front of the farmhouse and waited for his family to exit the residence.

His mother came to the door holding his baby sister. Little Hannah wore a lavender dress and white prayer *kapp,* and she was barefoot. "Have you seen Joseph?" his mother called.

"Not since breakfast," Jed replied. He wondered if he should get out of the vehicle and help search. He had just made up his mind to go when his *dat* left the house, followed by his twin brothers, Jacob and Eli, and their younger brothers Isaac and Daniel.

"Did you find Joseph?" Jed asked as his father approached the buggy.

"*Ja,* but he's managed to get his pants dirty. Your *mam* is making him change his clothes."

Jed's brothers Jacob and Eli climbed into the buggy's backseat. Samuel Lapp hoisted young Daniel into the buggy, urged him to sit between Eli and Jacob, and then offered his hand to Isaac.

"I can manage, *Dat,*" Isaac said as his father helped him into the backseat.

"*Ja,* I suppose you can, Isaac," Samuel said kindly, "but we're late leaving, and I'm expecting you'll have to find a quick seat and make room for Joseph. Hannah can sit on *Mam*'s lap."

Katie Lapp locked the house and approached with Hannah in her arms and holding five-year-old Joseph's hand. Joseph didn't look happy, but he was neat, clean and dressed properly, and his *mudder* was content.

"How nice you look, Joseph," Samuel said with a wink at his wife.

He hefted Joseph to sit between Isaac and Eli. The boys moved to accommodate their youngest brother. Samuel then took Hannah from his wife until Katie was comfortable in the front seat, then he handed back their daughter.

Jedidiah shifted to make room for his *dat*. "Visiting Sunday," he said with a smile as he picked up the leathers and spurred the horse on.

"Wait!" Katie cried, startling all of them. "The food!"

Jed laughed. "Not to worry, *Mam*. I took the salad and cake over to the Kings early this morning. They're going to bring them for us. I figured it'd be easier, and Mae offered yesterday."

Katie released a sigh of relief. "Mae does have the room since Charlotte married and Nancy left to visit relatives in North Carolina."

Hannah squirmed on Katie's lap, and automatically Katie shifted her daughter toward the window opening so that the little girl could look out.

"What kind of cake did you make?" Daniel asked his mother.

Katie straightened her *kapp*. "Upside-down chocolate."

"That's Noah's favorite," Isaac complained.

"It's my favorite, too," his father said, glancing back to meet Isaac's gaze.

"And mine," Daniel added.

"And mine," Eli said and Jacob agreed that it was his favorite, too.

His mother turned to eye her thirteen-year-old son. "You don't like chocolate upside-down cake?"

Isaac looked sheepish. *"Ja,* I love it." His cheeks

turned pink beneath his black hat, and he squirmed uncomfortably in his seat.

Jacob scowled and reached over Eli to jostle Isaac with his elbow. "Then why all the fuss?"

Isaac shrugged. "I was just saying that chocolate upside-down cake is Noah's favorite."

"And the favorite of most of us," Eli pointed out with a shake of his head and a small smile.

My favorite is cherry pie, Jed thought, and immediately an image of a young woman with red-gold hair and blue eyes came to mind. He frowned, forcing the memory away.

Conversation came to a standstill as Jedidiah drove toward the Mast farmstead. He enjoyed visiting Sundays. He wondered who'd be attending today. The number of families who came varied from Sunday to visiting Sunday. It was a perfect day for an outdoor meal. He'd tossed a ball into the rear of the buggy with the thought that there'd be someone willing to play catch on the lawn behind William and Josie's farmhouse.

The Masts' driveway loomed ahead and Jedidiah turned on the battery-operated turn signal before maneuvering the vehicle left onto the dirt path. Rosebushes lined the side of the driveway as they drew closer to the house. The scent of the pink rose-blossoms permeated the air.

Gravel mixed with dirt crunched beneath the buggy's wheels as they approached the house and pulled into the barnyard. The side lawn was filled with neighbors. Tables had been set up and covered with white-paper table liners.

"Looks like this will be a fine gathering," Samuel said as Jed noted the line of buggies parked on the grass and the folks in the yard. There were eight buggies. Theirs made nine. Nine families with numerous children. Plenty to play catch with or toss yard darts or any other game someone wanted to play, Jed thought.

"Look, there's Mae!" Katie said. "Jacob, would you please help her with the food? Take the cake and salad from her. It looks like she has enough to carry inside."

The King buggy was parked two vehicles down the row from them. Mae and Amos had gotten out of the carriage, followed by their sons John and young Joshua, who spied the Lapps and waved at them with excitement. Mae waved and grinned at Katie. Mae was Katie's closest friend and lived on the other side of the road from the Lapp farm.

"I'll go, *Mam,*" Eli offered. He got out of the buggy and headed toward Mae.

"Me, too," Jacob said as he followed closely on his brother's heels.

"Why don't you both go?" Jed suggested loudly with barely concealed amusement. There were no girls in the King family buggy. Why the hurry to help out?

Jed climbed down from the front seat and took Hannah from his mother. *Dat* got out after him and then assisted his wife.

"Jed-ah," Hannah said as she patted Jed's cheeks.

"*Ja,* Hannah banana?"

She laughed, a babylike chuckle that warmed his insides and made him smile. "I'm not Hannah-nana. I'm Hannah Yapp."

Jed kissed her baby-smooth cheek. "That you are, little one. Let's go, shall we? And see if we can find one of your little friends for you to play with."

"Morning, Jed, Samuel," Amos King greeted, and Jed saw that Samuel had caught up with him.

"Perfect day for a picnic," Jed said, smiling at his father's closest friend.

"Mae brought her famous sweet-and-vinegar green beans."

The Lapp men grinned in appreciation. "Katie made chocolate upside-down cake and ambrosia salad with extra coconut and marshmallows," Samuel said.

All three exclaimed with delight and then laughed. "You'd think we didn't often get such *gut* food, but we do all the time," Amos said. "Mae and Katie are the best cooks."

"Josie is a great cook, too," Samuel said. "I wonder what she's made for us today." The three men chuckled and continued on.

* * *

"Timothy, Thomas, I want you to behave today, do you hear?" Sarah stood over her young brothers, examining them with a critical eye. "We've only arrived at cousins Josie and William's two days ago. Don't make them sorry that we've come."

"We won't, Sissy," Thomas promised, and Timothy nodded in solemn agreement.

"Where are Will and Elam?" she asked, referring to Josie's six-and seven-year-old sons.

"Upstairs," Josie said as she entered the neat-as-a-pin kitchen. She grinned at the twins. "Go up and urge them to come down, please. They're taking entirely too long up there. I can only imagine what they're getting into."

Sarah liked Josie Mast from the first moment she'd met her. It had been a long time since her parents had taken the family for a visit. Sarah had been the youngest then at only four. William and Josie hadn't met and married yet. William couldn't have picked a better wife, Sarah thought.

"I appreciate you having us, Josie."

"'Tis my pleasure," Josie said, and Sarah could tell the woman was sincere.

Sarah looked about the kitchen, anticipating what needed to be done. There was nothing on the stove, as it should be, since it was Sunday. The white countertops were clear except for a stack of white napkins, plastic plates and utensils. The prepared food had been stored in the pantry and in the refrigerator. "What can I do to help?"

Josie adjusted her white apron before she opened the pantry door. "Besides the rooms you cleaned, the pies you baked and the salads you made yesterday?"

"That's not much work," Sarah said with a smile. "At home, my chores keep me forever busy. Here, I feel like I'm on vacation."

"Gut." Josie reached into the pantry and took out the two pies that Sarah had baked the previous day. "The salads are in the refrigerator." She leaned over to glance out the kitchen window. "It looks like everyone is almost here. Oh, the Lapps have arrived! There's Jedidiah carrying his sister, Hannah."

Sarah froze while retrieving the potato salad from the second shelf of the refrigerator. Heart beating wildly, she carefully put the bowl on the counter and then slowly, casually joined her cousin at the kitchen window.

Jedidiah Lapp? Was he the man who'd saved the twins and captured her attention back home? Josie shoved aside the white window-curtains.

And then Sarah saw him. It was Jedidiah. Carrying his little sister in one arm, Jed waved to family and friends with the other. He looked the same, only better.

Would he recognize her? Would he greet her as

if they'd met before? Or had he forgotten all about the girl who spent one Sunday afternoon and evening with him in Delaware?

"Here we go, banana," Jed teased as he set Hannah on a bench to play with her little friends. There was a pile of crayons on the table. One of the children had drawn a tree and a flower on the white table covering. "You'll watch out for her, Rosie?" he asked Mae and Amos's five-year-old granddaughter, Rose Ann.

Rosie turned large hazel eyes toward him. "*Ja,* we'll have fun together." The other children nodded. At the table with Rosie and Hannah were three-year-old Benjamin Stoltzfus and four-year-old Susie Jane Miller.

Satisfied that his sister would be content, at least for a little while, Jed headed toward the porch where William and the other men had taken up residence on white wicker rocking chairs.

"Food will be ready soon," Josie said as she came out of the house with plates, napkins and utensils. "Jed. Samuel. Amos. Glad you could make it."

"Wouldn't miss your fine cooking, Josie," Amos said.

"Can't say I did much cooking for this occasion. My cousin did it all. Sarah, come out and meet Samuel and Jed. Amos, I believe you met yesterday." Amos nodded.

Jed stood and turned as a young woman with red-gold hair and a familiar blue gaze exited the house, carrying a huge bowl of potato salad.

"This is Sarah Mast, our cousin from Delaware. Sarah, this is Samuel, and his son Jed."

Jed felt warmth curl in his belly. "Sarah," he said. "It's *gut* to see you again."

"Ja," she replied, her cheeks turning a bright shade of pink.

Josie looked stunned. "You've met?"

Sarah answered, "Jedidiah was the one who rescued Thomas and Timothy at Spence's."

Josie nodded as if she'd heard all about it. "The incident with the car."

"It's young Sarah with the twin boys!" Arlin Stoltzfus climbed the porch steps.

Sarah smiled. "It's nice to see you again, Arlin."

Jed, caught up in the wonderful sight of her, could only stare and listen. He'd thought of her often since he'd left Delaware for home. He'd never before enjoyed an afternoon as much as the one they'd spent together at the Millers' after-worship services.

Sarah Mast, Jed thought. She was a long way from home.

She met his gaze, and he smiled.

Chapter Six

"Sarah." Jedidiah studied her. "Is your family here?"

The look in his gaze thrilled her. Sarah liked the sound of her name on Jed's lips. She shook her head. "*Nee*—just the twins. *Mam, Dat* and my older brothers are at home." She looked away as she became overwhelmed by thoughts of her *mam*'s heart surgery. The procedure was scheduled for this coming week.

"Are you all right?" Jed asked.

She looked at him and smiled. "I'm fine."

He studied her a moment, clearly concerned. Suddenly, she felt him relax. "Come meet my family," he urged, as if eager to introduce them.

"I'd best check on my brothers first." She searched for the twins. "Have you seen them?" She heard shouts, giving away the boys' whereabouts.

"They're over there." Jed grinned as he pointed

to where the twins played with their young cousins. "They're having a *gut* time with Will and Elam."

Sarah nodded. Will and Elam were Josie and William's two youngest. "Do you think they can stay out of trouble long enough for me to meet your family?" she said with a smile as she regarded the exuberant boys fondly.

"Ja," Jed said. "They will be fine. Young Joshua King has been keeping an eye on them." He turned to regard her with amusement. "They will not get into trouble unless Joshua decides to join them."

Sarah widened her eyes. "Should I be worried?"

Jed chuckled as they approached the tables—and one in particular. "Joshua is a *gut* boy. They will be fine."

Sarah felt the barest touch of his hand brush her back as Jed steered her toward his parents.

"Mam. Dat. This is Sarah Mast. I told you about her." He gestured her closer. "Sarah, this is my *vadder,* Samuel, and my *mudder,* Katie."

Sarah nodded respectfully. "'Tis nice to meet you, Samuel. Katie." Jed's features, she realized, were a stunning combination of his parents'.

"You're William's cousin from Delaware." Smiling, Katie shifted to make room on the bench for Sarah to sit next to her.

"Ja." Sarah couldn't help smiling back as she sat down. "We've come for an extended visit. Josie has been kind to me and my brothers." She caught sight

of Timothy and Thomas running in their direction. "Here they come now."

Jed chuckled. "Timothy and Thomas are Sarah's young, *active* twin brothers."

"That is a nice way of describing them," Sarah said, but she watched with love in her heart as the twins approached.

"Jedidiah!" Timothy cried as they reached the table. "Do you want to play ball later?"

Jed nodded. "After we eat."

Thomas grinned. "Sissy, can we get our plates and eat with Will and Elam?"

"*Ja.* But mind your manners and eat your meat and vegetables before taking dessert."

"We will," Timothy said, and Thomas nodded vigorously in agreement. Timothy noticed some adults studying them. "*Hallo.* We are Sarah's brothers. I'm Timothy and this is Thomas."

Sarah caught Katie stifle a grin. "It's *gut* to meet you boys. I'm Katie, Jed's mother. Do you know that I have twin sons? Only, my boys aren't identical like you."

"You do?" Thomas asked.

"*Ja.* See those two down the table? The one with dark hair is Jacob. The fair-haired one is Elijah."

"Jacob. Eli!" Katie called. "Come meet these twin brothers."

Jacob and Eli rose from their seats and approached. Introductions were made, and it was clear that the older Lapp twin brothers had impressed the young Mast twin boys.

Seated with Jed's family, Sarah felt the warmth and love of the Lapps surround her. They made her feel welcome.

Katie Lapp looked much younger than Sarah's mother. With eight children of various ages, she had to be the same age or older than *Mam,* Sarah thought, but poor health had taken its toll on her *mudder,* making her look older than her early forties.

Jed's mother's sandy-brown hair peeked out from beneath the front of her white prayer *kapp.* She wore a dress of lavender with her white cape tucked in a white apron. There were soft laugh lines near the corners of her warm brown eyes and outside her mouth, which looked as if it curved upward often.

A woman who enjoys her family and her life. Sarah felt wistful. If only *Mam* felt well again… *Mam* had been full of life and laughter until she'd begun to feel ill. The exhaustion that had taken hold of her had stolen her strength and the worry had taken her smile.

Sarah closed her eyes briefly. *Please, Lord, help the doctor mend Mam's heart.*

"There's Hannah," Jed said, interrupting her thoughts as he pointed toward where his little sister played at a table with other young children. "She is growing up quickly."

"Ja," Katie said quietly. She addressed Sarah. "Hannah is my baby." She smiled brightly, and it was as if the sunshine had burst forth from behind a cloud. "My youngest and the only girl."

Sarah couldn't help grinning back at her, her brief moment of wistfulness gone. With Katie nearby, it was hard to feel melancholy. Jed's *mudder* reminded her of *Mam* during the early days, before and right after the twins' birth. "Hannah has many brothers to keep a watch over her," Sarah said.

"'Tis true." Katie watched her little daughter at ease with other children. "I suspect that she will be well able to handle herself as she gets older without her brothers' help."

A young couple waved as they approached. "This is my brother Noah and his wife, Rachel," Jed told her. "Newlyweds."

Noah and Rachel each carried two plates covered with plastic wrap. "Rachel's been baking again," Jed murmured, and Sarah looked at him for an explanation. "My brother loves dessert, and he has a special liking for chocolate. Rachel indulges him with brownies, cookies, cakes and chocolate-cream pies."

"It sounds like she loves him," Sarah said and then blushed at how her words could be taken. She stood. "I should get back to help Josie in the kitchen." She paused a moment to meet Jed's gaze. "We can talk later."

Jed's slow smile did odd things to her insides. "*Ja.* I want to know what you've been doing since I last saw you."

Sarah gave a silent nod. Then with a fluttering heart, she intercepted the young newlyweds and requested the dishes from Noah.

"I'm Sarah Mast from Delaware." Sarah introduced herself, and Noah relinquished the plates to her with a lazy grin. He was a good-looking man, with sandy-brown hair under his banded straw hat and in the short beard that edged his chin.

"It's nice to meet you, Sarah." Rachel, a lovely young woman with dark brown eyes, wore a blue dress under her black cape and apron. A white prayer *kapp* covered her dark brown hair.

"You've been visiting with my family," Noah said quizzically.

"*Ja,*" she replied. "Jedidiah and I met when he and Arlin came to the Sale at Spence's Bazaar back home in Delaware."

"Jed mentioned you," he said with an intent look that made Sarah silently wonder what Jed could have said to his brother.

"Go visit with your family," Rachel urged her husband as she cast Sarah an understanding glance. "Sarah and I will help Josie fetch the food."

His expression softened as Noah glanced at his wife. "Hurry back," he said in a soft, warm voice.

Rachel's dark eyes beamed with amusement. "Go sit with your *bruders* and behave."

Noah headed toward his family's table as Sarah and Rachel walked to the house. The day was warm and sunny. The sky was a glorious shade of blue without a single cloud in view. A light breeze made it a perfect day to enjoy a meal outside. Everyone was in good spirits, Sarah noticed as she and Rachel walked side by side across the yard and onto the front porch.

"You couldn't ask the Lord for a nicer day," Rachel said, as if reading Sarah's thoughts.

Sarah chuckled. "I was just thinking the same thing." She hesitated as she grabbed the screen door and opened it for Rachel to enter first.

"Congratulations," Sarah said, "on your marriage." And then she worried if she should have mentioned it, but she felt at ease in Rachel's company.

"I never expected to be this happy," Rachel replied with a gentle smile.

Sarah and Rachel exchanged grins. "Praise the Lord," Sarah said laughingly.

"Sarah!" Josie called. "Would you get the food from the refrigerator?"

"*Ja,* Josie," she called back.

"What can I do to help?" Rachel asked.

"Help Sarah" was Josie's answer.

Rachel followed Sarah to the gas refrigerator,

and Sarah bent inside to retrieve platters of cold meat and bowls of various salads, vegetables and puddings.

They chatted and laughed as they worked to bring all the dishes into the kitchen, where they set them on the counter. Several Amish women crowded into the room unwrapping the food to prepare it for the table.

"I remember when I first came to Happiness," Rachel said as they returned to the refrigerator for the last of the food. "Noah followed me back to the refrigerator to *help,* he claimed, during a visiting Sunday that was held at his house." Rachel's expression warmed with the memory. "I was upset with him at the time. I was bending inside searching for the potato salad when I heard his voice right behind me. I was so startled I bumped my head as I stood to confront him. He made me uncomfortable, and I wanted to run from him."

Sarah listened with interest as they stopped in the other room. "But you didn't—"

"Nee." Rachel chuckled. "I demanded the bowl back but he refused. He followed me outside and put it on the table. I was embarrassed—yet pleased. I shouldn't have been, but I was. I waited until he'd set the food down and then I left to return to the house. He stayed outside, and I was relieved. I never imagined that one day we would be man and wife."

Sarah tilted her head as she eyed Rachel with curiosity. "Why not?"

"'Tis a long story," the other woman said as she bent inside the refrigerator for the last bowl. With bowl in hand, she straightened and smiled at Sarah. "Would you like to come to our house and have tea one day this week? We can talk and get to know each other better. How about on Tuesday?"

Sarah was delighted. "I'd like that."

"Gut," Rachel said, looking pleased.

They returned to the kitchen, and Sarah grabbed two bowls to take outside. Rachel followed with two baskets of rolls and bread.

"Sarah, it wasn't long ago that I came to Happiness from Ohio, as the new schoolteacher for the community."

Sarah paused and looked back.

Rachel held her gaze. "There is happiness to be found in Happiness, Pennsylvania. I sense sadness about you. I believe you will enjoy your visit here for however long you plan to stay."

Rachel and Sarah carried the last of the dishes from the house. Sarah stopped. Jed had risen from his chair and was speaking with two young women.

"The Zook sisters," Rachel said quietly from behind her. "Anna and Barbara. Annie is the taller one and the eldest."

Sarah continued slowly toward the food table, trying not to glance toward Jed and the two women.

"Does Jed like one of them?" she asked Rachel, who set the dishes she carried next to Sarah's.

Rachel was quiet a moment. "Everyone thought for a time that Jed and Annie were sweet on each other," she finally said, her eyes focused on the young women, who remained deep in conversation with Jed.

Sarah glanced over, saw Jed's relaxed stance, then she quickly looked away. "Are they still seeing each other?" She waited with bated breath for Rachel's reply and finally faced her to read the young woman's expression.

"*Nee,* they have not been seen together in months. This is the first time I've seen them talking for any length of time. And Annie wasn't alone then. Barbara was with her."

Sarah wanted to study the three, but refused to appear too curious. What if Jed and Annie still cared for each other and had simply suffered a misunderstanding? She thought of her time with Jed, the light in his eyes when he looked at her. She didn't think Jed was thinking about Annie when he'd spent the day with her back in Delaware. How Annie felt was a different thing entirely.

"Let's go. Noah sees us and he is waving us over," Rachel said.

"I don't know.... I should sit with Josie and William," she began.

Rachel smiled at her knowingly. "It is up to you.

We'd like you to sit with us, but I don't want you to feel uncomfortable." She paused and then quietly added, "Look, the Zook sisters have left Jed's company."

Sarah saw with relief that Annie and Barbara had rejoined their family. "I'll take the meal with my cousins," she said, "and sit with you while we eat dessert."

"Gut," Rachel replied with a grin.

Jed was relieved when Annie Zook and her sister finally walked away from him. He saw Sarah and Rachel cross the yard, and he felt his day brighten.

Seeing Annie had been awkward. It should have been easy, as they were friends, but the fact that they had once almost been something more made him wonder if Annie had felt the same as he did when they'd discussed their friendship—or if she'd only agreed because he'd been the one to bring it up.

Annie had been pleasant, and he had detected no dismay for her sister in Barbara. They had chatted casually, talking about their families, the weather and their farms.

"Do you still have your dog, Millie?" he'd asked her.

"Ja, she is a joy to have in the house." Annie confessed that she was grateful that her parents allowed her to keep the dog inside. Animals were usually kept in the barn.

While he had nodded and smiled during the conversation, Jed had found his mind wandering back to Sarah. He'd caught sight of her and Rachel as they'd made numerous trips from the house to the food table.

Sensing Annie's gaze, he'd quickly smiled in her direction, and he'd realized that he'd given the wrong impression when he heard Annie's breath catch as their gazes collided.

Jed frowned. *We are friends, Annie. Nothing more. We'd agreed, remember? There is another waiting for you...someone to love you as you should be loved.*

He didn't love Annie Zook, and he wouldn't settle for anything but love.

"You've been busy," he said as he walked up to meet them, and Sarah nodded. "Are you hungry?"

"Ja." Sarah suddenly looked uncomfortable. "I should eat with my cousins, but I promised Rachel I'd eat dessert with your family."

"I'll see you later, then." He'd rather have her return to share the end of their meal than have no time to spend with her.

Jed rose and meandered over to the food with Noah and Rachel. He filled his plate with a mixture of delicious dishes before he returned to his family's table.

He heard Sarah's laughter as he ate. He flashed a glance toward the Mast family table, smiled when he saw her chuckling, probably over something that Timothy, Thomas and their cousins—Will and Elam—had said or done.

Sarah looked carefree and happy. The darkness that had once shone in her blue eyes had vanished. She didn't look his way, although he willed it. He would have to be satisfied that she'd come back to his table to eat dessert.

"I've enjoyed talking with you," Sarah said as she rose after they'd eaten dessert together. She'd chosen a piece of apple pie, while Jed had enjoyed a slice of cherry.

Jed stood. "Will you walk with us later?" he said, shooting Noah a glance.

"Ja," Noah added. "'Tis a beautiful day. Please join us." He looked at his wife.

"Ja, please do." Rachel flashed her a sincere, welcoming smile, her dark eyes crinkling with amusement.

Sarah grinned back. "I may do that, after I check with Josie to make sure she doesn't need me."

She cleaned up the food and packaged leftovers with the other community women. When she was done, she headed outside to find Rachel, Noah... and Jed.

The sun was warm on Sarah's face as she and the three Lapps walked across the lawn and into the farm fields. A robin flew from a branch onto the ground ahead of them, chirping to its mate still up in the tree.

Sarah watched with a smile as another bird sat on the ground close by, and the two robins rooted about in the dirt, before taking flight.

"Couldn't ask for a nicer day," Jed said.

"Ja," Sarah agreed. "'Tis a lovely day for a walk."

"We should have gone for a ride." Noah stopped a moment as if to enjoy the scenery. He raised his wide-brimmed straw hat before setting it onto his head again.

Sarah watched as Rachel stood nearby, smiling at her husband. While Rachel and Noah seemed aware only of each other, she felt someone's gaze and looked to see that Jed studied her with an odd look that made her wholly aware of him. "Anything wrong?" she asked, wondering if she had a speck on her nose or a crumb near the corner of her mouth.

He shook his head slowly, his gaze warming, his lips curving upward, as he continued to look at her. "I'm glad you decided to walk with us."

Sarah tried not to let his study unnerve her. "Seems too nice of a day to stay inside."

"Will you come for a ride with me one day?" he asked, his expression suddenly unreadable.

She didn't want him to realize how much she would enjoy such a ride. "If there is time—"

"There is always time, Sarah Mast. The Lord

gives us all we need. We just have to use it wisely."
He held on to her gaze.

And riding with you would be a wise thing to do?
She thought briefly of Annie Zook.

"Thomas and Timothy—" she began.

Jed smiled. "They can come with us."

His offer to take the boys warmed her. "We'll see
what our days bring."

"*Ja,* of course, Sarah," he said, his lips quirk-
ing with amusement. "Until then, I shall appreciate today and our time together."

Sarah didn't want to ponder the idea of a relationship with Jed Lapp too deeply. She would be
leaving soon—what possible chance would the two
of them have if Jed actually wanted a relationship?

"Sarah, look! It's a red fox and her cubs!" Rachel
cried suddenly, outwardly drawing Sarah's attention, but she remained overly conscious of the tall,
dark-haired man beside her.

"It's a large one," Sarah commented and flashed
Jed a look to see that his amusement had deepened.
*As if he suspects I like his company but am trying
not to show it.*

The two couples paused to watch the fox with
its cubs as the animals crept unaware of the hu-
mans. Suddenly, the mother spied their presence
and scurried her young ones into the brush away
from watchful eyes.

"Shall we continue?" Jed asked her several moments later, his deep voice close to Sarah's ear. "There is a stream up ahead. Maybe we'll find some wildflowers."

"*Ja,* let's keep going!" Rachel answered while Jed stood silent within inches of Sarah.

Sarah felt the light touch of Jed's fingers as he urged her in the right direction before he withdrew. Although he didn't touch her again, she could still feel the sensation of Jed's hand as she walked beside him with Noah and Rachel. During the rest of their walk, Jed kept his distance from her, which disappointed her. He seemed too polite as he walked a few feet from her side.

Had she misread his attention? Had Jed's thoughts turned to Annie Zook and their earlier conversation?

Sarah swallowed hard. She reminded herself that it would be best if she forgot Jedidiah Lapp and her growing feelings for him. Soon she'd be leaving Pennsylvania…and Jed would stay here in Happiness to marry and build a life with his new wife.

There was no hope for them.

Was there?

Chapter Seven

The day was sunny and warm, without a breeze to stir the leaves on the trees and the wet laundry that Sarah and Josie hung to dry on the clothesline.

"These wet garments will dry in no time," Josie said. She bent and pulled a shirt from the wicker basket. Shaking out the wet green fabric, she secured it to the line with wooden clothespins.

"'Tis not as breezy as yesterday," Sarah agreed, "but the temperature is much warmer." She withdrew a small pair of tri-blend denim pants and threw them over the line, pinning them in place before reaching into her basket for an identical pair. "It feels good to be outside."

"Ja." Josie smiled in her direction. "We've been lucky this spring. God has been *gut* to us all season."

Sarah nodded as she met her cousin's gaze. "We accomplished a lot this morning," she said, pleased.

"No more chores for you after this." Josie pinned

a blue dress into place. "You are having tea with Rachel later today."

"It will be nice to see her again." Sarah experienced warmth as she recalled how she and her new friend Rachel had become fast friends. "Is the *schuulhaus* far?"

"Nee," her cousin said. "It's to the right and down the road apiece. Take the buggy, though, since it will be afternoon when you get there. You may want to stay and chat until late."

"I'd rather walk." Sarah grabbed a small maroon shirt from her basket, shook out the wrinkles and then pinned it to the clothesline before doing the same with its twin. "'Tis such a nice day, and I can use the exercise."

"You can walk if you'd like," Josie said. "The sun stays out longer these evenings. You won't have to walk home in the dark if you're invited to supper."

"I'll be home in time to help you with supper."

"No need." Josie tucked a stray lock of hair beneath her *kapp*; the tiny strand had come loose during morning chores. "You've done more than enough since you've been here. Enjoy your time with Rachel."

"I don't feel right leaving you with the boys." Sarah frowned as she thought of her twin brothers. "What if they misbehave?"

Josie chuckled. "What're two more unruly children?" With the last garment secured on the line, she picked up her basket and regarded Sarah with an assessing look. "You need not worry, Sarah. If I can handle my youngest two, I can certainly manage the twins." She waited as Sarah retrieved her empty basket and moved closer to her before they headed back to the farmhouse. "They get along well, don't *ya* think? There has been little trouble with the four of them, which amazes me."

Sarah followed Josie up the porch steps, pausing on the last stair to lean forward and wipe her forehead with the back of one arm. She straightened her prayer *kapp*. "I did notice that they've been behaving lately. Do you think it's because they get tired with all the activity?"

Josie opened the screen door, and Sarah grabbed hold of the edge, allowing her cousin to precede her into the house. "*Ja*. They certainly go to sleep easily enough," the older woman said. "Not a peep out of them once they're in bed." Her tone softened. "I think coming here has been *gut* for your *bruders*..." Her tone softened. "And you."

"*Ja*. I'm grateful we had this chance to visit," Sarah agreed. "I only wish that *Mam* wasn't having surgery."

"I'm sure you'll hear from your *dat* as soon as he has something to tell." Josie entered the kitchen and set the laundry basket on the table bench.

"Josie, I'm frightened for *Mam*. I pray to the Lord daily but I'm still scared." She set her basket next to Josie's. "Does that make me an awful person? I know we should trust solely in the Lord's love, but this is *Mam,* and I can't help but be concerned."

Josie gave Sarah a hug. "*Nee,* you're not awful, Sarah. God understands that we are human. As long as we continue to pray to Him, He will be there for us. In the end, all will be well."

When her cousin released her, Sarah had tears in her eyes. "I hope you are right."

"The Lord loves us. He gave us life. He is there whenever we need Him. Rest assured that we are all praying for your *mudder.*" Josie studied her with understanding. "Before you leave, would you check on the boys for me? They are either upstairs or in the barn."

Sarah climbed the stairs to check their bedroom. The second floor was too quiet as she approached; the boys couldn't be up here. She heard laughter outside and peered out the open window. She watched as all four boys spilled out of the barn and gave chase to each other onto the lawn and then into the backyard. No matter how hard it had been to leave home, she realized, coming here had been the best thing for Timothy and Thomas.

And for her. If she hadn't come to Happiness, she never would have seen Jedidiah again.

It was one o'clock in the afternoon as Sarah headed down the dirt lane and onto the main paved road toward Rachel's cottage. Before she'd left, she'd washed and donned clean clothes. Her morning chores of scrubbing, dusting, washing and baking had left telltale dirt streaks on Sarah's face and arms and across her cape. As she turned right and then crossed the road to walk facing traffic, she softly sang a hymn from the *Ausbund*. Swinging her basket, she studied the surrounding countryside as she sang and walked toward the community *schuulhaus* and the teacher cottage currently occupied by Rachel and Noah.

It took Sarah a half hour of walking before she saw a glimpse of the *schuulhaus* ahead. She didn't mind the journey. It was too nice a day not to walk, and singing made the distance shorter. She smiled. She looked forward to seeing her new friend. She and Rachel had shared an instant liking for each other. Was it because Rachel, too, had come from a different state? The only difference was that Rachel had come to settle permanently in Happiness, while Sarah had come only for an extended visit.

Soon, she'd have to return home, Sarah reminded herself. Any day her family would be calling her and the twins back to Delaware. Everyone in Happiness had been so kind and caring that Sarah knew she'd have liked to stay the summer, if not for her worry for *Mam* and the knowledge that her *mudder* needed her.

Who was keeping house at home? Who was there

to clean and cook and feed *Dat* and her older brothers? Who was caring for *Mam* and making sure she had everything she needed? Who was available to her all day and night?

"Aunt Iva?" Sarah murmured. "Mary Alice?" She frowned. She should be there for *Mam*—not her aunt or cousin.

She stopped, closed her eyes and prayed. "Help me, Lord, to be a *gut* and dutiful daughter, to understand why I am here in Happiness with the twins instead of home in Kent County with *Mam* and *Dat*."

Sarah opened her eyes and continued down the road, aware of the sights and sounds of the spring season. Lush green grass carpeted lawns and extended yards, while pink, yellow and red roses grew in abundance along an *Englischer*'s driveway, the blossoms' sweet scent drifting to her nose. A child played happily in her front yard with a big yellow dog, while the girl's mother and father sat in cloth chairs, watching with fond smiles as they sipped from cans of iced tea.

She caught a glimpse of the *schuulhaus* ahead. Farther up the lane next to the *schuul* was the teacher's cottage—her friends' home.

The twins were doing well. *Thriving,* she thought with a slight smile. She was a dutiful daughter here where her parents wanted her. For now, she had to take solace that whatever happened at home, she had done the right thing and obeyed her parents.

Rachel opened the door as Sarah approached. *"Willkomm!"* she exclaimed. She grinned as she gestured Sarah into the house. "I'm so glad you've come. You walked?" she said with a smile as she turned on the gas stove under the teapot.

"Ja, it seemed too nice of a day not to." Sarah studied her surroundings, immediately liking the kitchen's cozy warmth. "Am I too early?"

"Nee." Rachel grinned at her as she set down two teacups with matching saucers on the kitchen table. "I've been eager to see you again."

"Me, too." Sarah handed Rachel the basket of treats. "Lemon squares." She paused. "For you. Someone told me that you liked them."

"I do." Rachel beamed as she accepted the basket, peeked inside to see the confectioner's sugar-dusted yellow squares. "But I didn't know anyone knew."

"Josie noticed you seemed to enjoy them during one visiting Sunday," Sarah said, glad that her cousin was an observant person…except when it came to guessing Sarah's own thoughts.

"I wonder what else she noticed," Rachel murmured.

Sarah shrugged. "I wouldn't know. Unless it pertains to William and her children." *Or the twins or me,* she mused.

The teakettle began to whistle, and Rachel removed it from the stove while Sarah sat down at the table. As Rachel made tea, Sarah unwrapped the lemon squares. Leaving the tea to steep, Rachel set out a sugar bowl, a jar of local honey and a small jug of milk. It was only after the tea was poured and flavored did Rachel pause to study Sarah. "How are you making out at the Masts'?"

"They've been wonderful to us," Sarah said. "I like Josie. She is *gut* for William and a fine *mudder* to her daughter and sons."

"*Ja,* I like her, too." Rachel took a sip of her tea and then cradled the warm cup with her hands.

Sarah reached over to select one of Rachel's chocolate-chip cookies. "Tell me about you and Noah. About how you met and later married."

Rachel smiled, but there was a brief glimpse of something painful in her dark chocolate-brown eyes. "When I first arrived in Happiness, I learned that everyone thought that Noah and my cousin Charlotte would wed one day. Noah rescued me from a runaway buggy my first day in Lancaster County. He was wonderful and brave. Charlotte was with him that day, and I thought they might be sweethearts. I tried not to like Noah, knowing that he belonged to her, but I couldn't help it. You've met Noah. He is just too likable."

Sarah chuckled. "It's obvious he loves you."

Rachel's features softened. "*Ja,* but I didn't know it then. I lived with Charlotte and her family when I first came here. Noah came to the farm often." She sipped from her teacup before she continued,

"I thought he came to see Charlotte. Noah and my cousin have known each other since they were infants, and it was obvious that they liked one another. Yet, once I moved into the teacher's cottage, Noah started to stop by at the cottage or the *schuul* instead, to ask if anything needed fixing or if I wanted help."

"Charlotte and Noah weren't sweet on each other?" Sarah asked, eager to hear more.

Rachel took a bite of a lemon square and a look of delight entered her expression. "This is *gut!*" she exclaimed before she went on. "They liked each other well enough. In fact, at one time, they did think about marrying, but then they realized that they didn't love each other that way. They were like brother and sister rather than sweethearts. Charlotte fell in love with and married Abram Peachy. I don't think you have met Abram yet, as the Peachy family is currently away visiting Abram's relatives in Indiana."

Sarah nodded. "And Noah?"

Rachel blushed. "Noah loved me."

"So all ended happily ever after," Sarah said with a smile.

"Not exactly," Rachel admitted. "You see, about a year and a half ago, I was in a buggy accident back home in Millersburg, Ohio. I was with a local boy, and the buggy slipped off the icy roadway and into a ditch when a car sped around a corner. Abraham was unhurt, and so was my brother, who rode with us as chaperone. I was in the hospital for a while. Abraham never came to visit me—not once—and I was heartbroken." She paused and drew a sharp breath. "I was severely injured—a broken arm, a couple of cracked ribs and…I hurt my abdomen." She closed her eyes a moment as if in pain. "The doctor didn't know if I'd ever be able to give birth, and although I loved Noah, I couldn't allow myself to care for him too deeply. He's good with children, Sarah. He should have a child of his own."

Sarah had felt a tightening of sympathy in her chest as Rachel told her story. "But you must have worked it out between you, since the two of you married."

"Ja." Rachel's lips curved into a soft smile. "Noah wanted me more than a child. But—"

Sarah sipped from her teacup and waited.

"I think I may be pregnant," Rachel confessed. "You're the only one I've told. I don't know for sure. I want to make certain first. I don't want to disappoint Noah—or his family."

Tears stung Sarah's eyes. She understood. There were other physical reasons that a woman might think she was pregnant and not actually be with child. "What did the doctor say…after the accident?"

Rachel's grin was wry. "That's it possible, but

not likely. If I do become pregnant, I'll be considered high-risk."

"Rachel, I'm sorry...." Sarah rose from her seat, skirted the table and hugged her friend. "You haven't seen the doctor yet," she guessed.

Rachel inclined her head. "*Nee*. Noah will want to go with me. I need to be sure before I tell him."

Sarah returned to her seat.

"I don't know why I find it so easy to talk with you," her new friend said.

"I feel the same way about you. I told you about *Mam*'s surgery the first day we met." She had told Rachel all about *Mam*'s illness while cleaning up after dessert that day.

"Have you heard anything from your family?" Rachel asked.

Sarah shook her head. "Not yet. It's too early. The surgery is tomorrow."

"I'll pray for her, Sarah," Rachel promised.

"And I'll be here if you need me for any reason... as long as I'm not called home."

The sound of a screen door as it was opened and shut was followed by Noah's deep voice raised in greeting. "Rachel!"

"In the *kiche!*" The light of love brightened Rachel's gaze as she stood and waited for her husband. As Noah greeted his wife, his brother entered.

Sarah felt Jed's presence keenly; he seemed to fill up the room. He looked wonderful in his work clothes. She tried not to notice how his suspenders fit over his green shirt or the strength inherent in his muscled arms bared beneath his short shirtsleeves. Her heart pounded hard as he smiled in her direction and they locked gazes.

"Sarah." He seemed to be genuinely happy to see her.

Her heart raced faster. "Jed," she greeted, wildly pleased to see him. Her nape tingled as he pulled out a chair beside hers and sat.

"Would you like some tea?" Rachel asked the two men.

Noah nodded. "*Ja*…and something to eat. Jed's helping me with a delivery, and since we had to drive past here…"

"I'm glad you did," his wife said happily. "Would you like a lemon square?" she asked Jed. "Sarah made them."

Jed's smile was slow and heart-stopping. "*Ja*, I'd like to taste one if Sarah made them," he said, while Noah reached for a chocolate-chip cookie.

Rachel poured each man a cup of tea, and Sarah watched as Jed added sugar but no milk. Sarah's gaze noted Jed's big, strong hands handling the teacup with extreme gentleness as he raised it to his lips. He captured her gaze over the rim of the cup, and Sarah looked away, embarrassed at having been caught staring.

"Well?" Rachel asked when Jed tasted a bit of a lemon square.

Jed turned to focus his gaze on Sarah. "Delicious," he said, and Sarah blushed but was unable to look away.

"Sorry, Sarah," Noah apologized, "but I'm partial to chocolate."

Sarah grinned at Noah. "So I've heard…" She chuckled. "And from more than one person."

Noah returned her grin. "Rachel's eyes resemble dark chocolate, don't *ya* think?"

"Noah!" Rachel blushed as she rose to put on the teakettle again.

Suddenly, Sarah's day brightened. She and Rachel enjoyed the brothers' company for the next half hour, and then it was time for the men to return to work. "That was unexpected," Sarah said once Noah and Jed had left.

"Hmm," Rachel said as she thoughtfully stared at the door through which the two brothers had departed. "Wasn't it just?"

That night, while she lay in bed with Ellen asleep beside her, Sarah thought back on the day with a strange sense of exhilaration.

She'd had a fine working morning, a nice afternoon tea at Rachel's, and…Jed had stopped with Noah to join them. *He likes my lemon squares.*

Sarah made a mental note to make more of them for Rachel…and for Jed.

Sarah knew she was foolish to feel this way about Jedidiah Lapp. She would be leaving soon and it was unlikely that she'd ever see him again. The thought made her stomach burn suddenly and her heart ache.

Why did they meet again if the Lord didn't have something in mind for them?

She closed her eyes and prayed silently, vehemently, for the Lord's guidance and help during the rest of her stay in Happiness. *Lord, help me to know what to do. If Your plan for me doesn't include Jedidiah Lapp, please keep me from losing my heart to him.*

Chapter Eight

"Sissy, can we visit the Kings with Elam and Will? Cousin William's going to take us." Timothy beamed up at her with blue eyes a shade lighter than hers.

Thomas stood beside his brother bobbing his head. "Please, Sissy."

Sarah stopped sweeping the front porch to lean on the corn broom's wooden handle. "Does Josie know?"

"Ja," Timothy said. "William's gonna help Amos at the farm, and he'll bring us home."

"Then you may go," she replied, holding back a smile, "but remember to mind your manners and behave."

"Ja, Sissy!" This time it was Thomas who spoke up. "Joshua has puppies in their barn."

Watching as the boys ran to meet their cousins, Sarah recalled the trouble once caused by the twins' fascination with dogs. She shuddered whenever she thought of the near-accident when they'd chased a puppy into the path of an oncoming car. *Thank Ye, Lord, for Jedidiah Lapp's quick response.* The boys could have been seriously injured or killed if Jed hadn't been there to snatch them out of harm's way.

Her thoughts turned to *Mam* as Sarah set the broom in motion again. It was Thursday, and *Mam* had had her surgery yesterday. *Is she all right? Have the doctors successfully repaired her heart? Why hasn't* Dat *called to let me know?* Surely he would have called if her mother had taken a turn for the worse.

When she finished sweeping the front porch, Sarah went into the house and confided her fears to Josie. "I'm worried about *Mam.* What if something terrible went wrong during her surgery?"

Josie looked up from the sink and the basin of sudsy water filled with the canning jars. "You must not fret, Sarah," she said. "Ruth's surgery might have been scheduled for late afternoon. If so, wouldn't Daniel want to check on her this morning before letting you know? He'll call soon."

"I hope you're right." Sarah leaned the broom in a kitchen corner. Earlier, she had swept the first-floor rooms. She would tackle the upstairs tomorrow.

"You'll see."

Her cousin's matter-of-fact tone made Sarah relax. She approached the sink where Josie worked.

"Shall I change the bed linens?" she asked. "Or do you want help here?"

"Bed linens. If you could start with the boys' rooms, that would be *gut*." The older woman grinned. "They'll be leaving shortly, and it will be quiet here today."

The corners of Sarah's lips curved upward. "A nice peaceful break from the boys?"

"For a short time," Josie said as she washed a jar, rinsed it in hot water and then set it on a clean dish-cloth spread out on the counter. "I will miss them soon afterward. I always do."

"I know what you mean." Sarah extracted clean pillowcases and sun-dried sheets from the linen chest. "They are so much a part of our lives."

With Josie's agreement ringing in her ears, she climbed the stairs and entered the bedroom shared by the four boys. The day was cooler than it had been, and the breeze blowing in through the open window past the plain white curtains was refreshing. Working quickly but efficiently, she stripped each bed. With skill born of experience, she remade the beds with clean sheets, deftly tucking the bottom corners in and fluffing the newly encased pillows before setting them in place. When she was done, she smoothed out the quilts that she'd replaced on both beds.

She gathered up the dirty sheets and started down the stairs. When she heard a deep voice near the front door, Sarah paused on the steps. She detected the words *Sarah* and *mudder* and *phone call*. Her throat constricting, she rushed with sheets over her arms toward the front door, where Jedidiah Lapp spoke with Josie in the hall.

"Mam?" she managed to whisper.

"Ja," Josie said. "Jed was at Whittier's Store when the call came. He's come to take you. Your *Dat*'s waiting for your call."

"I have the phone number where you can reach him," Jed said, his quiet tone full of concern.

She locked gazes with Jed. "Did he say anything?"

"Nee," Jed replied. "Bob Whittier said your *vadder* wanted only to speak with you."

Tears stung her eyes as Sarah nodded. "I should go." She looked about, feeling lost, wondering what to do with the sheets she had draped over her arms.

"I'll take those," Josie said softly before she disappeared with the sheets into another room.

"Danki," Sarah murmured. Her stomach burned and her heart raced rapidly with fear.

"Sarah," Jed urged gently, "we should go."

She shook herself as if she had been in a trance. *"Ja."* She'd been waiting to hear about her mother, and now she was afraid of what she'd learn. *Please, Lord, let* Mam *be well!*

A warm, masculine hand reached out for hers. "Are you ready?"

Jolted from her thoughts, Sarah gave Jed a little nod.

"Sarah, she will be fine," he said softly.

She took strength from his strong but gentle grip as she was led from the house and helped into the buggy before he released her hand. Soon, Jed was steering the horse and buggy down the lane and onto the paved road toward Whittier's Store.

They were quiet for a time and then Jed said, "Sarah—"

"She had surgery yesterday," Sarah told him. "Heart surgery." She looked at him with tears in her eyes. "I've been waiting to hear." She drew a sharp breath. "What if something bad happened during the operation?"

Jed reached over to briefly place his warm hand over hers, and the simple touch comforted her. "Sarah, let's see what he has to say. It may be Daniel wants to talk with you…to tell you himself that Ruth is fine and to ask about the twins."

Sarah gave him a weak smile. "I hope you're right." Despite her concern, she was conscious of Jed's warm, strong fingers against hers, and when he removed them, she felt the loss.

Jed studied Sarah with concern. The only sound for a time was the clip-clop of the mare's hooves on macadam and the occasional engine of a car as one passed from either direction.

"We're almost there," he said softly.

"Gut." She sighed wearily. "I shouldn't worry, but I can't help it." Her bright blue eyes glistened with tears as she met his gaze, and he wanted nothing more than to take her into his arms and comfort her. He was glad he'd been at Whittier's when the call came. Now he would be near if she needed him. *Please, Lord, let Sarah's fears be unfounded.*

Spying the store ahead, Jed turned on the signal and waited for a car to pass from behind before he steered the buggy into an empty spot near the hitching post in the paved parking lot.

He quickly jumped down, tethered the horse and hurried to Sarah's side with his hand extended to assist her from the vehicle. She accepted his help with a nod of thanks, and he walked with her into Whittier's Store, which was a combination general store, eatery and tack-supply shop.

Jed reached into his pocket for coins and pressed them into Sarah's trembling fingers. "There's the pay phone," he said.

"Danki," she whispered.

"Is this the young lady?" Bob Whittier asked, and Jed nodded. "No need to use the pay phone. You can use this one here." He gestured toward the phone sitting on the cashier's counter. "Don't matter if it's long-distance or not."

Jed watched Sarah lift the receiver and dial the

number he'd given her with a shaking hand. She looked anxious as she waited for someone to answer.

"Dat?" he heard her ask. *"Ja,* it is Sarah. How is *Mam?"* Jed stood by as she listened intently. *"Ja?* She will be all right?" She frowned and Jed moved closer as if he could infuse her with strength. "She will be in the hospital how long?" She met Jed's gaze as she nodded. "I see." She paused, listening. "We are fine. The twins enjoy spending time with Elam and Will. Josie has been *gut* to us." She paused to listen. *"Ja,* I will tell them." She closed her eyes briefly. "I love you, too, *Dat.* Please tell *Mam* I love her and I hope she feels better soon."

She raised a hand to tug on a *kapp* string as she clutched the telephone. *"Ja,* I will. Tell Ervin and Toby I miss them. *Ja.* I will. I will wait to hear from you, then. *Ja, Dat.* I will talk with you soon." She set the handset carefully back onto its cradle. She stood a quiet moment, lost in thought. She approached Bob Whittier. "I appreciate the use of your phone," she said.

"No problem," the old man said gruffly. "Feel free to use it whenever you need."

Jed studied Sarah and waited silently for her to talk with him as they headed outside together.

"Sarah—"

She turned to face him, and tears coursed down her face, wrenching at his heart and silently urging him to take her in his arms. He didn't. "What's wrong?"

She shook her head. "*Mam* came through the surgery. Her doctors think she will make a full recovery."

He stared into the depths of her glistening blue eyes and realized that what she felt was joy. Her tears were from happiness, not from concern, as he'd feared.

"That is wonderful, Sarah." He smiled and touched her arm before quickly withdrawing. "Come. I'll take you home. Josie will want to hear your news."

He helped her into the buggy, untied the horse and climbed onto the seat next to her. He flashed her a quick glance, but she was gazing out her side of the vehicle. With a flick of the leathers, he spurred the horse on, back toward the Mast farm.

"I appreciate the ride," Sarah said softly after a time, interrupting the quiet previously broken only by the sound of the horse's hooves on the road.

"I'm glad I could help." Jed enjoyed looking at her, but didn't look for long. He knew she'd be uncomfortable if she caught him staring. Turning his attention to the road, he still had a vivid mental image of her…the lovely color of her red-gold hair… the shining vivid blue of her eyes…the smoothness of her white skin…the pink of her perfectly formed, sweet lips.

"I'm happy that your *mudder* is doing well," he said.

"It was bad at first, *Dat* said, but she came through and the doctors are hopeful."

Bad? he wondered. How bad? He didn't ask. "She is awake and doing better?" He flashed her a look.

Her smile was genuine. "*Ja.* Much better."

Jed felt a relief so powerful that it was as if his own mother had been the one to undergo the surgery. What was it about Sarah Mast that made him feel this strong emotional connection to her?

He had no right to think of her as often as he had been, to consider a relationship with her. She'd be leaving soon, and he'd be staying in Happiness.

His thoughts turned solemnly to Annie Zook. He feared he'd hurt Annie when they'd ended their relationship and talked about staying friends. How could he trust his feelings for Sarah when he'd been wrong about him and Annie? If he hadn't seen how happy Noah was in his marriage to Rachel, he might have courted and wed Annie and been content.

But then he'd met Sarah in Delaware, and he'd begun to wonder, although he'd known it was foolish when they'd only just met. Seeing her in Happiness stirred mixed feelings inside of him. He felt happy when he was with her. When he was with her, the time flew and it was as if their moments together went by too quickly. He thought of what life could be if they were man and wife.

He silently scolded himself. He had to stop this.

Sarah had a family in Delaware, a mother who needed her help.

Jed was conscious of her beside him as he steered the horse down the road toward the Mast farm. It was quiet inside the buggy, but it wasn't an uncomfortable silence. For him, there was joy in being in her company, in accompanying her wherever she wanted to go.

The Mast farmhouse appeared ahead on the right, and Jed steered the horse onto the dirt driveway. He pulled the vehicle close to the house, jumped down, skirted the buggy and held out his hand to Sarah. He felt a jolt of happiness when she placed her fingers within his grasp.

Sarah smiled as she climbed down, and Jed felt his heart rate kick into high gear as she regarded him with warmth.

"*Danki,* Jed," she said softly as he reluctantly released her hand.

"I'm here if you ever need a ride." He gazed at her intently to gauge her reaction.

Her smile reached her eyes. "I will remember that."

"Sarah!" Josie came out of the house and onto the front porch. "How's Ruth?"

"*Gut!*" she called back. Sarah headed toward the house. She hesitated in her stride as if she'd realized that he hadn't followed her. "Coming?" she asked softly. "I thought we could have a glass of lemonade together."

"That sounds wonderful," he answered as he trailed behind her into the house.

"*Mam* is fine," Sarah told Josie as she approached the porch, conscious of Jed's presence behind her. She was glad when he followed her. She didn't want him to leave yet. It had felt good to have him near when she'd called her father. His presence, his kind words, had given her strength when she most needed it.

"Lemonade?" she asked Josie.

"*Ja.*" Josie called into the house, "Ellen, bring the pitcher of lemonade that Sarah made this morning." She smiled at Sarah and added to her daughter, "And some cookies, too!"

"Coming, *Mam,*" Sarah heard the young girl reply.

Sarah turned to Jed. "Would you like to sit inside or out?"

"On the porch," he replied, gesturing to a row of white wooden rocking chairs with white wooden tables between them.

"I'll help Ellen," Sarah said.

"*Nee,* you sit with Jed," Josie urged. "I'll go in."

Sarah sat in a rocker and Jed took a seat in the nearest one. "It is a lovely day," she said, "made better by the *gut* news about *Mam* I received today."

"Ja," Jed said quietly.

She flashed him a quick glance at his tone. He studied her with a look that stole her breath and made her stomach flip-flop.

This is Jed, she thought. *Why do I feel nervous around him? It's not as if I haven't spent any time with him.*

They caught and locked glances. Finally, Jed released her gaze. "Sunday service is at the Amos Kings," Jed murmured conversationally. "Charlotte and Nancy will be home by then."

"They are Amos and Mae's daughters, and Rachel's cousins."

Jed nodded. "Charlotte is married to Abram Peachy. He is a deacon. They and their five children have been visiting Abram's relatives in Indiana."

"Five children!" Sarah was surprised. When she'd met them, she hadn't thought Amos or Mae old enough to have a daughter with five children.

Jed's lips curved. "They were Abram's before they were Charlotte's." When Sarah frowned, Jed chuckled. "Abram was a widower. Charlotte loves his children as her own, but she hasn't given birth yet."

Sarah's eyes sparkled. "I see."

"Nancy lives at home with Amos and Mae, but she, too, has been away." He reached up and adjusted his banded straw hat.

"Here we are," Josie announced, carrying four

glasses and the pitcher of lemonade on a tray. Her ten-year-old daughter, Ellen, smiled as she brought out a plate of various cookies and set it on a table between Jed and Sarah.

"You baked these?" Jed asked the young girl.

Blushing, Ellen shook her head. "Sarah did. She helps *Mam* a lot."

"You help her, too," Sarah said gently, noting the girl's discomfort.

"Indeed she does," Josie said with a smile for her daughter. "Would you run inside and get some napkins?"

Ellen nodded and scurried away only to return seconds later with a stack of white napkins, which she handed to her mother.

They sat enjoying the lemonade, the cookies and the day.

Josie stood first. "I'd better check on the boys—"

Sarah rose. "I'll do it."

"Nee," her cousin said. "You stay and keep company with Jed." She flashed him a smile. "Give my best to your *mudder*."

Jed nodded. "I will."

Suddenly, Sarah found herself alone on the front porch with Jedidiah Lapp. As she looked out over the yard and barn, she was conscious of him studying her. She faced him to meet his gaze head-on. He smiled at her, and she felt her heart pound. "Is something wrong?" she asked.

Jed shook his head. "I was wondering if you'd be staying for the singing on Sunday."

She blinked. "I—I haven't thought about it."

"Think about it and come," he urged softly. "I'd like to take you home again."

She couldn't help it—the memory made her smile. She had enjoyed her ride with him after the singing that night in Delaware. She knew she'd enjoy riding with him again, but should she?

"We're friends, aren't we, Sarah?" he said, as if trying to convince her of the innocence of his request.

Friends? Sarah thought. Yes, they were friends, but there was more…something she didn't want to ponder on too deeply. *"Ja,"* she said, "we're friends." As he and Annie were friends? she wondered, not liking the thought.

"Then you shouldn't be concerned with riding home with me."

"I'm not—" she began and then stopped, sighed. "I will come to the singing and ride home with you—" she hesitated "—unless you change your mind and want to take someone else home instead."

"Not likely," he said softly as he stood. "I have to get home. *Dat's* waiting for me—"

Sarah hadn't thought of Jed's plans for the day or how she might have ruined them. "I'm sorry—"

His chestnut eyes twinkled. "Don't be. I'm not." He reached out and tugged on her right *kapp* string.

Then with both hands, he adjusted her *kapp,* after which he cradled her head for several long seconds before letting go. Sarah could still feel the warmth of his fingers on her skin beneath the fabric.

"I will see you soon, Sarah," he said. "I enjoyed the lemonade and cookies."

"I'm glad you were there with me when I made the phone call." She was sure that he had no idea how much his presence had helped her through the difficult time of not knowing the outcome of her mother's surgery while they were on the way to Whittier's Store.

"It was my pleasure to take you, Sarah Mast."

With those words ringing in her ears, she watched Jed descend the porch and hurry toward his buggy. He climbed aboard, picked up the leathers and then waved before he drove on.

She'd never felt this strange in anyone's presence. She liked him—how could she not? But there was something more lurking inside her: fear, happiness, resignation. She was afraid that she was falling hard for Jedidiah.

But she was even more afraid that nothing could ever come of her feelings for him. Soon her family would call her home, and she would again be the dutiful daughter available to help *Mam* with the kids, the house and the chores.

Chapter Nine

The storm began with a distant rumble of thunder and a flash of lightning through the window glass. As the thunder strengthened, Sarah glanced over at the young girl in the bed next to her and saw that Ellen slept on peacefully.

There was no sign of Timothy or Thomas; no doubt they were sleeping, as well.

Sarah lay in bed, watching the play of bright light as it flashed through the window and onto the ceiling. She didn't mind the storm; she enjoyed the sound of rain on the roof, the droplets that spattered against the house. What she didn't like was if the lightning got too close or the thunder too explosive. Lightning could cause fire, and fire could cause loss of life and property. This storm was soft and easy, and it was just how Sarah liked it.

As the rain began to patter against the farm-house, Sarah found her thoughts shifting in different directions. She thought of home and her family, her mother in the hospital, her *dat,* her older brothers, her sister, Emma, and her husband, James, in Ohio.

Was *Mam* getting better? It had only been two days since she'd spoken with *Dat.* He would have called again if something terrible had happened. Wouldn't he?

Sarah closed her eyes and said a silent prayer that her mother would continue to improve until she was well again. Thoughts of *Mam* brought her around to her presence in Happiness. She had enjoyed her time here. She had taken on some of the chores for Josie, who was appreciative. When Sarah had offered to do more, Josie had declined, saying that Sarah did more than her share of work, that she should take time to have fun.

Take time to have fun? It had been a long time since Sarah had done anything but chores…except during that one evening back home at the Millers', when she'd attended a singing and Jed had taken her home afterward.

Sarah smiled into the darkness. It had been a wonderful night. She had enjoyed her time with Jed. She'd never felt so lighthearted, so alive, so happy, and it was Jedidiah Lapp who'd made her feel this way.

When he'd left for his home in Pennsylvania, Sarah had never expected to see him again. She'd known that he lived in Lancaster County, but the county was huge, home to the largest Amish population in the country. She'd realized that the odds of seeing him in Lancaster were slim.

Prior to her departure from Delaware, when her thoughts had been concerned with her *mudder,* had she really given Jed much thought? Perhaps as a passing musing, but nothing more. She hadn't wanted to hope…

But that first Sunday when she'd discovered that Jed lived in Happiness, that he was a member of the same church district as her cousins, she'd been at first stunned and then inordinately pleased. Her pleasure became tempered by the fact that someday soon she would go home to Delaware, while he would remain here in Happiness.

Back home, she had suffered some heartbreak after Jed had left, but with God's help she was able to find the strength and determination to return to her life, a life in which she did all the chores, working from morning until night when she'd drop into bed, exhausted. It was only after she'd awakened first thing the next morning, ready to start her day again, that her thoughts would return with a pang to Jed. Another prayer to the Lord, and she was able to continue with her day with the peace of knowing that Jed was out there somewhere, living his life, alive, healthy, happy.

Tomorrow was Sunday services, and the singing for young people was in the evening. Jed had asked her to go to the singing, then to ride home with him afterward. Sarah smiled with delight. The prospect of riding alone again with Jedidiah Lapp filled her with joy.

She shouldn't allow herself to feel this way, but she couldn't help it. *Please, Lord, help me to choose the right path.*

The rain fell in torrents, pounding the house, creating a ruckus, but Ellen slept on and Sarah smiled at the deep sleep of a child.

She heard a soft tap on the bedroom door. Or did she imagine it? The tapping came again, louder. *Timothy? Thomas?* Sarah rose to open it.

Josie stood at the door, a stack of towels in her arms on which lay a flashlight. "Sarah, I'm sorry to bother you, but we have a problem with leaking windows when it rains this hard. William is planning to replace those windows. We've been waiting for the new ones to come in." She handed Sarah the folded towels. "Would you place these around the windows and on the floor? Here's a flashlight."

Sarah nodded and accepted the stack and the flashlight, which was turned off.

Josie hesitated. "Did I wake you?"

"Nee," Sarah assured her. Josie looked like a young girl in her nightgown with her hair unbound and flowing well past her shoulders. With-

out thought, Sarah touched her long golden-red hair self-consciously.

Josie smiled at her and thanked her for taking care of the windows. "I'm glad I didn't wake you."

"The boys are still asleep?" Sarah asked, knowing that Josie would have checked on the boys before coming here.

A lightning flash lit up Josie's grin. "Sound asleep. They did their chores and played hard yesterday."

"Ja." Sarah grinned back at her cousin.

The women exchanged good-nights, and then Sarah turned on the flashlight and went to the first of two bedroom windows. The windows were indeed leaking. A small bead of water ran from over the windowsill, down the wall and onto the floor. Sarah leaned the base of the flashlight against the wall and placed the towel stack within easy reach. She dried up the wet areas before she packed towels into the crevice between the window and the sill. When she was done, she laid the remainder of the towels on the hardwood floor.

The storm was beginning to pass. Satisfied that she'd done all she could to stop the leak, Sarah went back to bed and her thoughts returned to Jedidiah Lapp and the happy knowledge that tomorrow she would see him again.

Sunday morning began as a clear day, which quickly turned cloudy and proceeded to a driving rain that threatened all plans for any outside activity. Taking the Mast open family wagon was out of the question. The Mast family, including Sarah and her two young brothers, climbed into the buggy. The vehicle with its three rows of seats had been custom-made for when William's parents—Sarah's grandparents—were alive.

William and Josie sat up front. The four boys sat in the second seat, while Sarah sat in the farthest buggy bench next to Ellen in the back. Enjoying the ride despite the rain, Sarah wondered how much the weather would affect the day's events. Would service and the meal be in Amos King's barn?

Sarah had her answer as William drove the buggy down the King driveway toward the house. She saw several people dash from their buggies through the rain into the house. The service was to be held in the King farmhouse.

Soon, Sarah and her family joined the others inside. Furniture had been cleared from the large living room. Benches stood in place, ready for the services to begin. Mae King handed towels to the newcomers so that they could dry off before taking their seats.

A group of three men stood to one side, deep in discussion. Were they church elders? She knew back home in Kent County there was often some discussion to decide who would handle the services on a particular Sunday.

"The one in the middle," a familiar male voice said in her ear, making her gasp, "that's Abram Peachy. And that—" a long, masculine arm reached past her shoulder to gesture toward a young blonde woman on the other side of the room "—is Charlotte, his wife."

The moment she'd realized who stood behind her, Sarah's heart had leaped for joy. "Rachel's cousin," she said breathlessly. "Who is that next to her? Nancy?"

She could sense Jed's grin before she turned to face him. As their gazes collided, he nodded. "*Gut* guess."

Sarah felt a tingling along her nape as she gazed up at the man before her. She could drown in the depths of his eyes. Stunned by her reaction to him, she quickly glanced back toward the women across the room. Forcing herself to concentrate on what she was seeing rather than the man next to her, she watched the interaction between the Peachys and Nancy King.

Mae King joined her two daughters with a smile on her face. Sarah realized that Charlotte and Nancy looked a lot like their mother. "Mae looks happy to see them," she murmured. She frowned as her thoughts turned toward her own recovering mother.

Jed was quiet a moment. "Your mother will be all right, Sarah," he said softly, as if reading her thoughts. "You've done a fine thing by listening to your elders, despite your feelings about leaving home."

"If something happens," she began, knowing that she couldn't have done anything but listen to her parents.

He shifted closer, until their shoulders almost touched. "Then it is God's will."

She looked at him. His expression was filled with understanding and something more. She quickly glanced away.

She saw church members take their seats. "Time for services," she murmured. She started to move and join the women.

"Sarah." Jed's voice was the barest threat of sound. "With this weather, some of the day's events might be changed."

She wondered if he referred to the singing.

He nodded as if reading her thoughts. Sarah tried not to feel disappointment. There was still the midday meal to share with friends and neighbors. Just knowing that Jedidiah was here brightened her day, made her thankful to the Lord. "I understand," she said.

As the service began with this day's officiate, Abram Peachy, the deacon, Sarah offered up praise and thanks to God. Her mother had survived the surgery, and for however long she had here in Happiness, the Lord had brought Jedidiah back into her life.

The service seemed to fly by, and then suddenly the men were shifting benches in the room and the women were in the kitchen unwrapping the food.

"Sarah," Rachel said. "These are my cousins, Charlotte and Nancy. Cousins—" she grinned "—this is Sarah Mast, William's cousin from Delaware."

"*Hallo,* Sarah," Charlotte greeted, her expression warm. "How do you like our village of Happiness?"

"I've enjoyed my time here."

Nancy beamed as she greeted her. "I'm glad to be home. I know our *grosselders* enjoyed the trip to North Carolina but there is no place like Happiness. They are over there." She pointed to an older Amish couple. "Harley and Emma King."

Just then, four young boys burst into the kitchen. "Elam! Will!" Josie scolded.

"Timothy and Thomas!" Sarah added. She pointed toward the other room, where tables had been set up with benches. "Go and sit now!"

Sarah gave the three women she was with an apologetic smile. "My brothers and cousins."

Charlotte grinned. "I can see the family resemblance in your brothers."

"Ah, my red hair!" Sarah chuckled.

"Sarah." A male voice spoke from behind her.

"*Hallo,* Jed," Charlotte and Nancy said in unison.

"Charlotte, Nancy." He nodded toward each one. "Rachel." He paused. "May I borrow Sarah?"

Sarah blushed while the cousins nodded and eyed her speculatively. Despite the strangeness of his approach, she couldn't help but feel a tiny bit pleased that Jed had sought her attention.

She followed him off to one side. "Is something wrong?" she asked him.

He hesitated. "I… Bob Whittier just dropped this by." He held out an envelope toward her.

"On a Sunday?" she whispered.

"*Ja.* He received the mail late yesterday. It was mixed up with his. He was afraid it was important."

Heart pounding within her chest but for another reason now, Sarah accepted the envelope, read the name and return address. "It's from Ervin."

Jed nodded. *"Ja."*

Suddenly nervous, Sarah tore open the envelope. She scanned the page, reading her brother's hand, and then smiled.

Jed watched as Sarah read the letter. "Is everything all right?"

Sarah met his gaze and grinned. "Everything is fine. *Mam* is doing well. She will be coming home next week."

Did he say anything about you going home? Jed wondered silently. He wasn't ready for her to leave. They had only just met up again. He didn't want to be nosy but he needed to know. "Did he mention anything else?"

"Only that they are managing well. Aunt Iva and my cousin Mary Alice have been helping out in the house." She glanced down at the letter and then returned her gaze to Jed. She grinned. "Remember the two girls my *bruders* took home? They've been stopping by with food. Often." She laughed outright, and the sound lifted his spirits. "Ervin doesn't seem pleased by the frequent visits."

Jed understood the feeling. If it wasn't the right woman, then it might be overwhelming if she kept coming around to "help" out. *Not that I wouldn't be anything but kind to her.*

"So your family is managing," he said. "They have the help they need and all the food they could want."

Sarah nodded as she continued to study the letter. "It seems so."

"Gut!" He was glad it wasn't bad news for her. "Sarah—"

She looked up from the letter to meet his gaze. The impact of vivid blue stole his breath. *"Ja?"*

"There may still be a singing this evening, but with the rain, we may have company when I take you home."

Was that a flicker of disappointment in her gaze? "It's fine, but I didn't realize that you lived so close, Jed. I can get a ride with the Zooks."

"I want to take you home, Sarah." He wanted to

do more with her—take long walks, spend hours talking with her, sharing a meal, holding hands.

"That sounds *gut*," she said softly. "As long as it's not an inconvenience."

"Being with you is never an inconvenience, Sarah Mast," he admitted quietly, and the truth struck him full force. He had come to care a great deal about her. He just didn't know what he was going to do about it.

The men sat and ate first. When they were done, the women and children enjoyed the meal. Today was more formal than last Sunday, when everyone shared tables outdoors.

Soon, church members cleaned up and began to leave. Most families were eager to get past the rain and into the warmth of their own homes.

"You will come to the singing if we have it?" Jed asked.

Sarah nodded. She studied his expression but noted nothing unusual on his features.

"I can speak with the Zooks to arrange a ride in for you," he said.

She shook her head. She decided that riding with Annie Zook wasn't a good idea. "I'll see if William can drop me off. If not, I'm sure Josie will arrange something."

Josie and William were ready to go. Sarah helped to round up the four boys and Ellen, and soon they were on their way home.

It wasn't until they were inside the farmhouse that Sarah spoke with her cousin.

"There is a singing tonight," she began.

"Ja," Josie said. "You will go. William will take you. I'm sure you can get a ride home."

Sarah nodded. "Someone already offered to take me home."

Josie opened her mouth as if to ask who, but then she abruptly closed it again as if she felt she shouldn't ask.

Sarah was relieved. Her feelings for Jed were too new. She realized what it meant to ride home with a young man. But she didn't want to discuss it yet.

As it happened, a fierce thunderstorm rolled in, canceling Sarah's plans.

"I'm afraid there won't be a singing tonight," Josie said as she glanced outside at the intermittent bolts of lightning.

Sarah hoped that Josie was right. She certainly didn't want to go out into the storm, but she didn't want to miss an occasion to spend time with Jedidiah.

A clap of thunder startled her. If it frightened her, what would it do to a horse on the road? As she backed away from the kitchen window, Sarah felt the envelope in her apron pocket—Ervin's letter.

It had been kind of Jedidiah to bring it to her. It was nice of Bob Whittier to see that it got delivered on a Sunday. The Happiness community had been wonderful. She was enjoying her time here, and so were her twin brothers. She'd never seen them so happy and active, and such sound sleepers once they were tucked up in bed at night.

The rain continued well into the night, the storm rolling out and then back in again. Sarah said a silent prayer that the wind, rain and especially the lightning did no damage.

She couldn't sleep, so she decided to use the time to write her family. She turned on a flashlight and wrote separate letters to *Mam, Dat* and Ervin. By the time she was done, it was late. The rumble of thunder grew distant, leaving only the gentle patter of rain on the roof above her, and Sarah grew sleepy. Thoughts of Jed entered her mind. When would she see him again?

Next Sunday, she thought, which was a visiting Sunday, if not before.

She recalled his deep, soft voice in her ear, the muscular arm that pointed over her shoulder, the light brush of his arm against hers as they shared a view.

She was in trouble. Jedidiah Lapp was taking up a lot of space in her mind these days, and she didn't think that was wise.

Sarah was carrying clothes downstairs to be laundered when William walked into the house, followed by Samuel, Noah…and Jedidiah Lapp.

'Josie!" William called. "We're putting in the new windows and doors today."

Josie came out from the back of the house. "*Gut.* Any more rainstorms like the last couple, and we'll be needing boats instead of towels."

As she descended the stairs to the last step, Sarah caught Jed's gaze. His lips tilted upward. His eyes gleamed. He looked handsome dressed in a maroon shirt and tri-blend denim overalls. His black-banded straw hat sat on his dark hair with the brim pushed back, and she felt the full impact of his unshadowed gaze. She could feel her face heat as she greeted the men, before she hurried down the hall toward the gas-powered washing machine.

She lifted the machine's lid, and as she was stuffing the wash into the basin, she was overly conscious that Jed was nearby. She heard the rumble of male voices outside the nearest window, saw Noah and Samuel carrying a new windowpane toward the area below the old one and set it down on the lawn.

Sarah watched Noah and Samuel Lapp walk past outside, perhaps to fetch another window.

Where was Jed? Working at the front of the house?

She poured liquid laundry detergent into the bottle cap and then spread it over the dirty clothes. She turned on the machine and felt satisfied when she saw and heard the spray of warm water.

A light tap on the window drew her gaze. Jed

pressed his face against the glass, his mouth curved in a wide grin.

Sarah laughed. She couldn't help it. There was something so playful about him; he made her feel good to be the focus of his attention.

He stood back and waved for her to come out. Should she go? She shook her head. She had chores to do.

He remained determined as he continued to gesture her outside.

Finally, Sarah shrugged, set the laundry basket on the floor near the washer and then stepped out into the bright morning sun—and into the direct line of Jedidiah Lapp's vision.

Chapter Ten

"Hallo." Jed gave her a tender smile.

Her heart skipped a beat. *"Hallo."*

"I didn't get a chance to talk with you since we made plans for the singing. I'm sorry it was canceled."

Sarah nodded. Should she confess that she was sorry, too? "That was a little more rain than I would have been comfortable driving in."

"Ja." He reseated his straw hat onto his dark brown hair. There was a tiny bead of moisture on the side of his face, and Sarah watched as he reached up to wipe it away.

She hesitated, unsure what to say. "I have work to do."

"I do, too," he murmured.

She heard a shout from the other end of the house. "My brother," Jed said. "I should go see what I need to do." He started to turn.

"Jed?" Sarah waited for him to stop.

He spun back and met her gaze. "It was nice of you to offer to take me home after Sunday singing, even if we never got to go."

His eyes brightened and his grin widened. "There will be other singings, Sarah." And he left to return to work with his father and brother.

"If I'm still here for another singing," she whispered, wondering when her family would call her back to Delaware.

Ervin had written that *Mam*'s recovery would take time and that it was a great thing that the twins weren't at home to disturb her.

I may be here for another singing after all, she thought with gladness as she reentered the house to check on the laundry.

Sarah heard the men working as they pulled out the old windows and replaced them with the new. When the front door was removed, the four young boys in residence thought the open space a play pathway for running in and out of the farmhouse.

"*Schtupp,* boys!" Sarah scolded as she came out of the laundry to spy what they were doing.

Noah peered through the open doorway and grinned. "I know a way to keep them busy."

Sarah raised her eyebrows. "How?"

"They can pick up the wood scraps and set them in piles away from the house."

She smiled. "And won't they be underfoot while you're creating the scraps of wood?"

"*Nee,* I'll suggest they help Ellen feed the animals first."

Sarah laughed. "This will be interesting," she said before she turned away.

Jed heard her laughter as he rounded the house. He loved the way it sounded—pleasant, girlish, full of happiness. He'd like to hear her laughing more. If it had been anyone other than his brother Noah who had made her laugh, he might have not been so pleased. *Nee,* that wasn't right. Jealousy was a sin and not permitted. Nor was envy.

He reached Noah just as Sarah left. "You said something to amuse her, I take it?" he said.

Noah's warm brown eyes twinkled. "I told her I had a plan to keep the young ones busy so that they wouldn't be in our way."

Jed's lips twitched. "And what was that?"

Noah told him, and Jed laughed outright. "This should be interesting." Jed regarded his brother with amusement.

Noah frowned. "That's what *she* said."

As it turned out, Noah's plan to have the boys pick up wood scraps didn't materialize until much later in the day. With some instruction, they did go to the barn to help Ellen feed the animals and milk the cows, and then it was time for lunch and the young ones gathered at the Mast kitchen table to eat. Sarah took sandwiches and desserts outside to the men, who sat on the front porch enjoying glasses of iced tea that Josie had brought out to them earlier.

She handed Noah his plate first. "Ham sandwich on homemade German rye bread with Swiss cheese. Just a hint of mustard." She gestured toward the dessert on one corner of the plate. "Chocolate cake," she said, recalling his love of chocolate, and Noah grinned.

Next, she handed Jed his sandwich plate but his dessert was cherry pie. He glanced down at the pie, then looked at her with a grin.

She nodded. She'd remembered that it was his favorite.

Josie had brought out lunch for William and Samuel. The men sat on the porch and enjoyed the meal. When they were done, they were back at work, determined to install all the windows and doors that were to be replaced that day.

As she moved about the house and yard doing chores, Sarah was overly conscious of the men's voices as they worked, of the sound of hammering as they secured each window after they'd set it into place.

Sarah hung laundry, dusted and swept the rooms downstairs, and when she was done, she headed upstairs to clean the boys' room. She entered the bedroom to find Samuel and Noah inside at the window opening. Startled by their presence, she froze and watched as Noah and his father tugged on a rope to hoist a window up into place.

Noah held on to the window frame as Samuel untied the rope and dropped it to the ground. Then the younger man helped to fit the window more firmly into the opening.

Sarah heard a noise against the side of the house.

"Careful, Jed. Make sure it's secure. We don't want *ya* falling, now."

"Ja, Dat," she heard Jed say.

"I'll hold it steady." William's voice reached up from ground level.

There was the clink of shoes against metal as someone—Jed, she thought—climbed the rungs of the ladder.

Suddenly, he was there, in the window opening, grinning. He didn't see her at first. The men exchanged instructions, and soon the window was secure, and Jed was ready to climb down. It was as he started down that he saw her.

He lifted a hand to wave. *"Nee!"* she cried. "Hold on!" She didn't realize that she'd spoken out loud until the two men in the room turned to stare at her.

"Sarah," Noah said, "we didn't realize you were behind us."

"I didn't want to disturb your work." Sarah was glad to note that Jed once again put his hands on the ladder as he continued the climb down.

Noah narrowed his eyes as he studied her. "He's fine," he said, his voice quiet. "This isn't his first time on a ladder. Jed knows what he is doing."

She bit the inside of her mouth. "Is that the last of the windows?" Seeing Jed on the ladder had made her nervous. She felt foolish for unintentionally revealing her thoughts.

"*Ja.* All done." Samuel checked the window and then turned, appearing pleased. "We did a *gut* day's work today."

"*Ja,*" Noah agreed as he slipped his hammer into the metal ring on his nail bag.

"I had no idea you could do all that in one day," Sarah admitted. She set the laundry basket on a bed and began to extract the boys' clothes. She placed them in piles, each one belonging to a different boy.

"We had a *gut* crew of workers," Noah said with a smile.

She nodded. "How is Rachel?"

"Wondering when you'll come for another visit." His eyes twinkled teasingly. At that moment, she could see his resemblance to his older brother.

"Tell her I'll come this week. Is there a day that's better for her?"

"*Nee.*" He glanced down to straighten his nail bag before looking up. "She'll be pleased to see you whenever you can come."

"Wednesday?" Sarah suggested, allowing Rachel two days' notice before she stopped by.

"Wednesday sounds *gut*." Noah looked pleased. "I'll tell her."

When Sarah ventured downstairs a while later, the Lapp men were getting ready to depart. She stepped out onto the porch to discover William and Josie chatting with Samuel, Jed and Noah. She quickly hurried inside and filled a plastic bag for each Lapp man with cookies, zucchini bars and fudge. She raced back through the house and slowed her steps only as she neared the front door—newly installed by the four workers.

"Here's a snack for the way home," she said as she distributed the bags of treats. All of them looked pleased as they accepted her offering, especially Jed. His look of pleasure made her stomach flutter.

After parting words, the Lapps moved toward their wagon.

"Jed." Josie called him back. "Would you wait a moment until I get something for Katie?"

"Ja." Jed approached until he reached Sarah's side, where he waited while Josie hurried back to the house. Sarah felt his presence keenly, the height and strength of him, his muscled arms developed no doubt by hard manual farm or construction labor.

"'Twas *gut* to see you again, Sarah," Jed said softly.

Sarah flashed a glance at Noah and Samuel, who were looking over some papers with William. "You worked hard today," she said.

He shrugged. "One day of work is like another."
He hesitated a moment. "Sarah—" he began ear-
nestly.

"Here it is, Jed!" Josie returned, interrupting,
making Sarah wonder what he was about to say.
Josie carried a clear bag of what appeared to be
pieces of evenly cut fabric. "Quilt squares," she
explained. "I've put them in a plastic bag for you."

"They're beautiful," Sarah said. "I haven't seen
these before."

"We hope to hold our quilting bee next week.
Katie is keeping all of the squares for us. We'll
meet at her house—yours," she said to Jed with a
smile, "next."

At Sarah's insistence, she allowed her to take a
closer peek.

Sarah saw that the fabric squares had been sewn
in the Amish star pattern. "May I help?" she asked.
It had been a long time since she'd had the pleasure
of attending a quilting bee.

"We'd love the help." Josie turned to Jed. "Are
you free tomorrow?"

"What do you need?" he asked.

"I need a few things from town. Would you mind
taking Sarah to pick them up for me?"

Jed's eyes lit up with delight. "I'd be happy to."

"I'll get my list," Josie said before she again disappeared inside.

"We can make a day of it," Jed told Sarah while they waited for Josie's return.

"I don't know if I can," Sarah replied, although the idea tempted her. Josie had never mentioned needing any supplies.

"We can take the twins with us."

"That would be *gut*," she replied. "I worry that they'll misbehave if I'm not around to scold them."

"Who?" Josie said as she rejoined them.

"The twins. We thought we might take them with us." Sarah was startled when her cousin disagreed.

"I have plans for the boys tomorrow," Josie replied.

Plans? Sarah thought. What plans did Josie have that would involve four active young boys—the twins and Josie's two sons?

"You can take Ellen if you'd like," Josie suggested. "She would enjoy the outing."

"*Gut!* We'll do that," Jed said. He turned toward Sarah. "What time can you be ready?"

"Whenever you'd like to leave—"

"Nine o'clock?"

Sarah nodded. "Then I can help with the morning chores."

"Sarah," Josie said, "no chores for you tomorrow. You'll be doing the shopping—that is work enough." She addressed Jed: "Eight o'clock?"

"I'll be here." A small smile played about Jed's lips. "Sarah, I'll see you tomorrow, then." With their plans for the outing made, Jed joined Noah and Samuel in the wagon and moments later the men left, leaving William to return to the house.

Sarah watched as Jedidiah drove off, her heart beating with excitement about tomorrow's outing.

"Here." Josie held out the list toward her. "Jed will take you wherever you need to go."

"I didn't know you needed supplies." Sarah studied the list, noting the baking and cooking ingredients. There were also a few other household items that Josie apparently needed.

"I meant to tell you earlier. William is busy or I'd ask him to take you."

"I have money. I'll take care of this for you."

"*Nee,* Sarah. You'll keep your money and take ours to buy the supplies."

Sarah sighed, knowing that it was useless to argue with Josie, who looked ready to do battle. "Are you sure you don't mind having the twins? They can be a handful."

"They behave well with my two," Josie assured her. "I have a few chores for them, which I'm sure they'll enjoy. Don't worry about them." She paused a moment. "Ellen will be excited to go. You don't mind having her?"

"Of course not!" she exclaimed as she and Josie headed into the house. "I enjoy Ellen's company. She is not wild like my dear twin *bruders.*"

"It will be *gut* for her to have a day out, as well."

Concern entered Josie's expression. "She is quiet at times. I worry about her."

"She is fine, Josie. I've seen her with the boys. She isn't quiet when she's with them. I've watched her on Visiting Sundays. The *kinner* like her." Ellen played well with the other children. Sarah wanted her cousin to know that her fears were unfounded.

Josie beamed. "I'm glad."

"If I'm to be out and about tomorrow, I'd best get back to my chores."

"You've done plenty today already," her cousin insisted.

Sarah shook her head. "*Nee.* I need to finish up in the house and then I'd like to work in the vegetable garden. It's a beautiful day, and it will be nice to work outdoors."

The next morning, when she heard the sound of horse hooves and metal wheels turning on dirt, Sarah went to the window and saw Jed pull up his family's market wagon near the front door of the farmhouse.

He looked up as if he knew she was at the window and waved. She lifted a hand in response before she turned toward the young girl seated on the bed behind her.

"Ellen, are you ready to go?" she asked with a smile. She had rolled and pinned up the young girl's hair only moments before.

Ellen nodded as she reached back to tie her black apron strings. Sarah saw her struggle for a few seconds before she offered to help. Ellen turned and Sarah made quick work of it, and then stood back to eye the girl appraisingly.

"We'll have a *gut* time today." Sarah checked her cape and her own apron ties, glad to find everything in place.

"*Ja. Mam* says we'll be going to lunch."

Sarah inclined her head. "Maybe we'll have a snack, too."

Ellen grinned. "Ice cream or kettle corn?"

"I like both," Sarah said with a smile.

"Me, too." Ellen preceded Sarah out of the room and down the stairs.

Jed was waiting for them on the porch when Sarah stepped out of the house first.

"*Gut* morning," he greeted.

"It is, isn't it?" Sarah couldn't keep the wide smile from her face. She'd looked forward to the day since she'd first learned of the outing yesterday.

"Is Ellen coming?" Jed ran his gaze over the length of her.

"*Ja*," Sarah said, noting his look, which thrilled her. She then moved to allow the young girl to step forward from behind her.

"*Hallo,* Ellen," Jed said softly. "Are you ready to have a wonderful day?"

Ellen nodded vigorously. She wore a green dress

with a black full-length apron, unlike Sarah, who wore a black cape and half apron tied at the waist over a royal-blue dress.

"We'll have a meal and a snack later," Jed said, causing Ellen to grin and glance toward Sarah, who returned the smile.

Josie stepped outside as Jed helped Ellen onto the wagon before he held out his hand to assist Sarah. "Have *ya* got the list?" she asked.

"*Ja,*" Sarah said. "Can you think of anything else you want to add?"

"*Nee,* I think that's everything." Josie shaded her eyes from the sun with her right hand. "Mind Sarah while you're out," she told her daughter.

"*Ja, Mam.*" Ellen turned to Jed. "May I sit in the back?" she asked.

"I don't see why not." After shoving a toolbox out of the way, Jed helped Ellen to sit in one corner of the wagon with her back against the rear of the front seat. A blanket cushioned the wood behind her. Then he climbed up onto the seat beside Sarah.

Sarah noted the power in Jed's arms as he flicked the leathers to spur the horse on.

"Are you ready?" he asked casually. "Is that your list?"

She nodded. "*Ja.* Josie needs baking supplies, some herb plants for her vegetable garden, and she wants some fabric for the quilt." Sarah glanced over in time to see Jed nod.

"I know where to go." He turned from the road to gaze at her from beneath his wide-brimmed banded straw hat. "Where would you like to eat?"

"You know the area better than me. Why don't you choose?" Josie had given her money for the supplies and for lunch for all three of them.

They drove in silence for a time. Sarah was conscious of Jed beside her and Ellen behind her.

"Look!" Ellen exclaimed. "That horse!"

Sarah frowned as she realized what Ellen had seen. "Jed—"

"I see it," Jed said as he pulled the buggy off the road and onto the driveway that led to a farmhouse. "It belongs to David Troyer, one of our church members." He stopped the buggy and got out. There was a horse caught in fence wire.

"Wait in the buggy," Jed said. "We don't know how he is going to react when I try to free him."

Jed approached the animal carefully. He didn't want to frighten it. He wanted the horse to stay calm while he reached over and freed its leg.

He hunkered down to study the situation. As he moved closer to untangle the mare's leg, the animal whinnied and moved anxiously. Jed stepped back.

"I don't want to frighten her," he said as he continued to study the situation.

"Jed," Sarah called out softly, "may I help? I can calm the horse while you work to get her free."

"How do you know it's a mare?" he teased. He looked at her and grinned before his expression became serious as he examined the animal. "I'd appreciate the help. Do you think you can stroke and soothe the horse while I try to free her?"

"Ja," she said. She addressed Ellen: "Stay in the buggy." Jed saw Ellen incline her head.

"Gut girl," he heard Sarah say.

She climbed down from the buggy and hesitated before she approached. "Do *ya* have anything to cut the wire if necessary?"

Jed frowned as he thought for a moment. "There may be something in the toolbox in the back of the wagon."

"I can look in the toolbox," Ellen offered softly.

"What do you need?" Sarah asked.

"Wire cutters or a razor knife." He waited with an eye on the horse for Sarah to reach him.

"Will these work?" Ellen held up a pair of tin snips.

Jed nodded. "Sarah, do you think you can get to the other side of the fence?"

There was a pause, and he looked over to see Sarah gauging the fence as if to decide the best place to enter the farmer's pasture.

"There," he suggested. "There's a gate there. You'll be able to get in as long as it's not locked."

Sarah hurried toward the gate. "It's latched but not locked. I can get in." She proceeded to slip inside the fence, shutting the gate behind her, before she carefully approached the horse.

"Can you get next to her?" Jed asked. He watched Sarah with concern. If anything happened to Sarah...

"Ja." She moved closer and the horse stirred restlessly. Sarah soothed her with soft words and gentle strokes along the animal's neck. With Sarah's help, the mare calmed and then stood docilely while Jed cut away just enough wire with the tin snips to free the horse's leg.

"Come on, girl," Sarah said, urging the mare away from the fence once she was free.

"Her leg is scratched but I don't think it's serious," Jed said. "Still, her wound needs to be tended. We'll ride up to the house and tell David. Sarah?"

"I'm coming," she assured him. He heaved a silent sigh of relief once she returned through the gate and joined him outside of the fence.

Chapter Eleven

Sarah was impressed with how quickly and efficiently Jed had freed the animal. The animal had been in pain, but she was obviously a good workhorse.

"I'll go up to the house," Jed said after driving the wagon up into the barnyard. He climbed down from the vehicle. "I'll be right back."

And then he disappeared from Sarah's view as he went to speak with the horse's owner, David Troyer.

He was back within minutes with a young man Sarah recognized immediately. She had seen him at Sunday church services. He had a wife and three children, although he couldn't be more than twenty-one years old.

"*Hallo,* David," she greeted.

"Sarah," he said with a nod. "You helped my horse. *Danki.*"

Her eyes met Jed's briefly. "I'm glad I could help."

"Ellen," David said, acknowledging the young girl.

Sarah smiled as Ellen said *hallo,* then the two men moved aside to talk quietly.

Soon, Jed climbed into the wagon next to Sarah. "He is going to see to his mare. I think she'll be fine."

"Ja," Sarah agreed.

"Now, Ellen, Sarah, are we ready to begin our day?"

"Ja!" Ellen exclaimed, and Sarah and Jed grinned at each other.

"Let's go, then!"

They went to the fabric store first, where Sarah bought Josie's quilting fabric. Sarah purchased three yards of three different colors—blue, burgundy and green—as well as three yards of unbleached muslin. While she was there, she purchased material for a new cape, apron and prayer *kapp* for herself and her mother.

Thoughts of her mother gave her pause. How was *Mam* faring? Should she ask Jed to take her to Whittier's Store so she could call home? Their neighbors, the Johnsons, would get a message to *Dat*…

"Sarah." Jed's voice interrupted her thoughts. "Are you ready for a snack?"

"A snack?" she echoed.

"Ja." His eyes lit up boyishly, and Sarah couldn't help but smile.

"Before lunch?" There was something so appealing about Jed as he stood there with Ellen by his side. He had a hand on the young girl's shoulder. She glanced toward Ellen to see that her eyes were lit up, as well.

"What are *ya* thinking?"

"Ice cream," they chimed in together.

"Ice cream." She saw their faces, and suddenly the thought of ice cream before their midday meal sounded like a wonderful idea. Sarah laughed. "Ice cream sounds *gut.*"

Jed grinned. Ellen exclaimed with joy, and then Jed took Sarah's fabric purchases from her and set them in the wagon before the three of them climbed in.

Jed drove them to a small ice-cream shop that had more flavors in one place than she'd ever seen. Back home in Kent County, Delaware, Sarah's favorite place for ice cream was Byler's General Store. Most of the time, her family kept ice cream in their gas freezer, but there was something special about going out for it. Today, she realized, that something special was Jedidiah Lapp driving her around town.

As she and Ellen sat across from Jed, Sarah enjoyed her treat and thought how fun it was to be eating it before the midday meal. They chatted conversationally while they ate, and then when they were done, Jed took them to a grocery store next, where Sarah bought all the baking and cooking supplies that Josie had requested. She spied fresh cherries in the produce aisle and decided to buy some to make a couple of chocolate-chip cherry pies, one for the family and one for Jed in appreciation for taking her into town.

Sarah paid for her purchases while Jed was wandering the store, gathering supplies for his mother. The cherries were bagged before Jed rejoined her, and she was glad because she wanted it to be a surprise.

"Did you get everything you needed?" Jed asked as he and Ellen approached.

"Ja," she said. She hesitated. "Do *ya* think we can stop by Whittier's Store?"

Jed smiled. *"Ja.* Would you like to make a phone call?"

Sarah nodded.

"We'll stop for lunch and to buy some kettle corn," he said with a smile at Ellen as he spoke. "Then we'll stop by Whittier's on the way back."

Seated across from Sarah as they enjoyed a midday meal, Jed found that he liked looking at her. She looked lovely in her royal-blue dress with black cape and apron. The small glimpse of hair pulled back from her forehead before it was hidden beneath her *kapp* was like spun gold that glistened with red warmth in the sunshine. He liked her company. If he wasn't careful, he'd find himself falling in love with her, but she would be leaving, and it would be wrong to start a relationship when they each had their lives in different Amish communities.

That doesn't mean I can't enjoy being with her now, he thought.

"I've had a *gut* time," Ellen said after she'd chewed and swallowed a bite of pizza.

"I have, too," Sarah said, and Jed felt enormously pleased that she had enjoyed the day as much as he had.

Soon, Jed was steering the horse into Whittier's parking lot. He climbed out and then held out his hand to Sarah. His heart skipped a beat as Sarah accepted his help and he felt the warmth of her fingers.

She stood waiting while Jed reached up and lifted Ellen down. Then the three of them went inside the store.

"Sarah." Bob Whittier greeted her. "Come to make a phone call?"

"May I?"

The man nodded. "Of course."

As Sarah went to the phone, Jed and Bob Whittier chatted about the weather and the comings and goings of the Happiness community.

Ellen wandered about the store, looking at all the items that lined the shelves.

Sarah dialed the phone number where she could leave a message for her father and waited for someone to pick up. She kept an eye on Ellen as the phone rang on the other end of the line. She was about to hang up after several rings, when someone answered her call.

She recognized the voice as that of John Jacobs, the owner of the convenience store closest to Sarah's home. "*Hallo,* John? This is Sarah…Sarah Mast. I'd like to leave a message for my family."

"Sarah!" John exclaimed. "You called at the right time! Your brother Ervin is here in the store now."

She heard John call Ervin's name and then there was a rustling noise on the phone as John handed the handset to her brother. And then Sarah heard the wonderful sound of Ervin's voice.

"Sarah!" he exclaimed. "What a surprise! Is everything all right?"

"*Ja,* everything is fine," she assured him. "I'm calling about *Mam.*"

"Sarah," Ervin said, because he knew his sister well, "try not to worry. *Mam* is doing well. Resting as the doctor ordered. Iva spent the night the day *Mam* came home from the hospital, and since then, she and Mary Alice have been by daily to help out. Mary Miller and some of our other neighbors have been bringing food by for us. Lots and lots of food," he added, sounding amused.

"That's *gut,*" Sarah said, glad that everyone at

home was being taken care of. "Will you tell *Mam* that I love and miss her?"

"Of course, Sarah," he said softly, "but she knows." Ervin was silent a moment, as if he understood how hard it was for her to be away from home. "Are the twins behaving?"

"*Ja,* they are enjoying their time here."

"I'm glad," her brother said. "They will remember their adventures there."

"*Ja,*" she agreed. *Just as I will,* she thought, thinking of her cousins' kindness, the warmth of the Happiness community—and her time with Jedidiah Lapp. Sarah stared at a bulletin board in the store as she and Ervin chatted for a minute more to catch up. "I'd better go, Ervin," she said as her gaze caught sight of the clock on the wall above the bulletin board. "Bob Whittier has been kind enough to let me use his telephone. It's not a pay phone." She paused. "I liked receiving your letter. I'll write to you and *Mam.* I think she might like that."

"She will," Ervin assured her.

After ending their conversation, Sarah hung up the receiver. "Thank you for the use of your phone, Bob," she said as Bob came to the counter to wait on a customer. "I hope I haven't stayed on too long. I can pay you for the phone calls."

"No, Sarah. It's fine," the storeowner assured her. He lowered his voice. "I have unlimited phone service, but don't tell anyone." The last was said with a twinkle in his dark gaze.

She grinned. "I won't tell." After Bob assured her that she could come back to use the phone anytime she needed it, Sarah turned to search for Jed and Ellen. She caught sight of Jed first. He was outside the store, talking with Annie Zook.

Jed's former sweetheart. She felt a burning in her stomach. He and Annie were smiling as they chatted. She heard Jed laugh out loud and saw Annie grin. Sarah suffered a little pang in the region of her heart as she turned to look for Ellen. She didn't have far to look. Ellen stood eyeing a display of candy and other treats. Pushing thoughts of Jed and Annie from her mind, Sarah smiled as she went to see whether or not Ellen would like any candy.

"Do you think the boys would like some?" she asked as she reached the young girl's side.

Ellen met her gaze as she inclined her head. "*Ja*. Can we buy some flavored sticks and some licorice?"

"Pick out whatever you think the family will like, and we'll purchase some treats for them." Sarah still had some spending money of her own. There had been little need to spend it since she'd arrived in Happiness.

Sarah paid for the treats and then glanced over at Jed to see if he was ready to go. Although he was talking with Annie, Jed sought her out with his gaze. Her heart gave a little jump.

Encouraged, Sarah urged Ellen to follow as she approached Jed and Annie with a smile. "*Hallo*, Annie," she greeted.

Annie nodded. "It's *gut* to see you again, Sarah."

"Annie and I were just talking about visiting this Sunday," Jed said. "The social will be held at our farm this weekend."

Sarah smiled. "Is there anything I can do to help?" The community women often came by to help the hosting family get ready for the onslaught of guests.

"Would you make some of your delicious pies?" Jed asked.

Annie's expression gave no indication of her thoughts. "I've heard about your pies, Sarah," she said politely after a lengthy pause.

"I bake much like everyone else," Sarah said, uncomfortable with Jed's praise.

After another awkward silence, Annie said directly to Jed, "I'll stop by to see if your mother needs my help."

Feeling out of place, Sarah decided to wait by the wagon for Jed to finish his discussion with Annie Zook. She bid Annie farewell and returned to the vehicle with Ellen, giving Jed a few moments alone with his friend.

Jed joined them not long afterward. He grinned

as he climbed onto the seat next to Sarah. "Are you ready to head back?" he asked.

"Nee!" Ellen exclaimed, and Jed laughed. The young girl leaned over the bench seat from the back of the wagon. "I had fun today."

"I did, too," Sarah said softly.

"Me, too," Jed said, his expression warm. Apparently unaware of her dismay, he picked up the reins and flicked the leathers. Under Jed's guidance, the wagon moved across the parking lot until it reached the main road. Jed looked both ways for any oncoming traffic. He waited as a car raced closer. "Would you like to do this again another day?"

"Ja!" Ellen answered, but Sarah remained silent. She didn't know how much longer she'd be in Happiness. And the mental image of Jed talking and laughing with Annie Zook still upset her.

"Sarah?" Jed asked with concern. Although the car had passed, he didn't spur the horse onto the roadway.

Her eyes met his. "I don't know how much longer I'll be here," she finally explained.

Jed frowned. "Did you learn something distressing from back home during your phone call?"

She shook her head. *"Nee. Mam* is doing well. I was able to speak with Ervin. I suspect that it won't be long before I get a phone call asking me to come home."

"I hope not too soon," he admitted as he studied her intently.

She blushed and looked away. "I have enjoyed my time here in Happiness." *And spending time with you.*

Jed checked the road again before driving the wagon forward. He drove on in silence for a time before an animal crossed their path and he had to pull up on the reins to slow down the horse. "We may have to arrange another outing sooner rather than later," he said.

Sarah bit down on her lip, then released it. "It's nice of you to say so."

"It's not nice of me at all," he admitted. "'Tis how I feel." And with that remark, he turned his attention toward steering the horse down the road toward cousin William's farm.

When her day with Jed came to an end, Sarah felt disappointed. Jed was quiet as he drove the vehicle down the lane into the barnyard near the farmhouse. He stopped the wagon, jumped down and then extended a hand toward her.

Sarah silently accepted his help, nodding at him in thanks before he turned to assist Ellen. He helped to carry in Sarah's purchases. Ellen tagged along behind them, bringing in the treats she had picked out for the boys and her family.

"How was your day?" Josie asked as Sarah entered the house.

"We had a nice time," Sarah said.

"A nice enough time to go again?" Jed queried with a hopeful smile.

Remembering him with Annie, Sarah was saved from replying at all when the twins and their cousins burst into the kitchen from outside.

"Jedidiah!" Timothy exclaimed. "I didn't know you were here. How come we didn't get to go into town?"

"Timothy!" Sarah scolded with a stern eye. Timothy wasn't fazed by his sister's tone.

"I had jobs for you to do," Josie said. "I needed you here."

"Ja!" Timothy said with bright eyes that lit up as if he'd suddenly remembered how he'd spent his day.

Thomas spoke up next. "We got to feed and brush the horses." He looked as if he'd enjoyed the chore.

"Ja! I like brushing the horses, but I needed help reaching the top of them, so William got me a stool to stand on."

Sarah smiled to see her young brothers' excitement. "I think you boys had a *gut* day right here."

They nodded vigorously. "We did," Thomas said.

Sarah smiled as she reached out, straightened Thomas's hat.

"Sarah." William came from outside behind them. "A letter came for you in the mail."

"A letter?" She had just spoken with her brother. He hadn't mentioned another letter. She accepted the envelope from William and stared at the return address with surprise. "It's from P.J. Miller," she said as William walked past and into the other room.

"P.J. Miller, my cousin?" Jed asked with a frown, and Sarah nodded.

She carefully undid the envelope flap and slipped out the letter. She unfolded the sheet of paper and began to read.

"Is everything all right?" Jed said with an odd tone in his voice.

"*Ja.* He is just writing to let me know how everyone is doing. He asked how I was and…" Her voice dropped off. She was surprised to hear from him.

"What else did he say?" Jed asked.

"He said that he—and everyone—misses me." P.J. was a friend and a nice man, but why should he miss her?

Jed listened to Sarah explain what was in the letter, and as she talked about P.J., he felt a burning in his stomach. He remembered his cousin's obvious interest in Sarah. P.J. was a good young man, and he knew that his cousin would treat Sarah right, but although he knew he shouldn't be upset, Jed found that his feelings for Sarah had grown the past few weeks.

"Are you going to write him back?" he asked her.

"I suppose I should. He took the time to write. I owe Ervin and *Mam* letters, as well."

"He likes you," Jed said, his mind still on his younger cousin.

"Who?" she asked distractedly.

"P.J." He studied her closely. There was nothing in her expression that gave away her thoughts or her feelings for P.J.

"I like him, too," she finally said. She watched as he set the packages he carried on the kitchen table. "He is a *gut* friend. Would you like a snack?" she asked.

He couldn't help but chuckle. "How could I possibly be hungry?" He regarded her with amusement.

Her eyes widened a second and then she laughed. "You're right. Ice cream, kettle corn and lunch." A beautiful smile played about her lips. "Would you like a drink, then? Lemonade? Iced tea?"

"Iced tea." He wanted to spend a few extra moments with her, and he didn't want to think about why.

Josie entered the kitchen. "Iced tea? Is there enough left for two more glasses?"

Sarah, who had retrieved the tea from the refrigerator, nodded. "There's plenty. I made more than one pitcher early this morning."

Jed watched as Sarah poured glasses of iced tea for Ellen, Josie, William and him, before pouring one last one for herself. He studied her hands, the careful way she took on the task. *She has nice hands,* he thought, *and a pretty smile.* She handed out the glasses and then suggested they sit on the porch to drink their tea.

He felt as if he could do this every day and evening as long as she was on the same porch with him, enjoying a bite to eat, a drink or simply some conversation.

He had a sudden mental image of Sarah sitting beside him on the front porch of a farmhouse, her face aged but still lovely as they watched a group of red-haired children playing out in the yard.

Jed mentally scolded himself, *What are* ya *doing?* Dreaming about something that will never happen.

Or would it?

After they finished their tea, Jed rose. "Time for home," he said.

"It was a wonderful day," Sarah murmured.

He grinned. *"Ja."* He stepped down from the porch and then turned to regard her with a feeling of inner warmth. "I will see *ya* on Sunday." She nodded. "Take care, Sarah."

"You, too," she said.

As he drove home, he took the memory of her sweet smile to last him until Sunday.

Chapter Twelve

During the days that followed the outing into town, Sarah found her thoughts returning again and again to Jed. What was it about him that had her envisioning her every moment with him? Yes, he was good-looking, but it was more than that. He had a kind heart. He had saved the twins, and he had taken the time to listen to her and be there for her whenever she needed someone.

Sarah frowned as she went about her chores on Wednesday morning. As she set the stainless-steel bucket under the cow's teats, she thought of her life back in Delaware, her family, who needed her, especially *Mam*. Soon she would leave. Soon she would get a phone call or letter that told her that it was time to go home. She wanted to see *Mam*, to see for herself that *Mam* was well. She wanted to see *Dat* and Ervin and Tobias.

As she milked the cow, she was barely aware of

the sound of milk squirting into the metal bucket. She was torn. She wanted to see *Mam,* but she wanted to stay. She missed her family, but she knew that as soon as she left Happiness, she'd leave a large part of herself behind. Her heart.

The existence of Annie Zook in Jed's life made it hard, but Sarah kept recalling how his gaze had sought her out while he was talking with Annie. Was that an accident? Or something more?

By Thursday morning, Sarah was no closer to feeling any better about the situation. The twins were happy and healthy. Josie seemed to enjoy having them around. William was kind, a good husband to Josie, and Ellen, Will and Elam were well-behaved children who were loved by their parents.

"What's wrong?" Josie asked as she and Sarah pulled weeds from the vegetable garden.

"Why should something be wrong?" Sarah replied as she tugged on a clump of grass that had sprouted between green-bean plants.

"You've been quiet."

Sarah stood and wiped her moist forehead with her arm. "I'm listening to the silence," she said. "Hear the bees? And I can smell the honeysuckle. It's a nice day and I'm simply enjoying it."

Josie rose to her full height and captured Sarah's gaze. "I know it's more. You may be enjoying the day, Sarah, but I also know that you've been quiet

ever since you came back from town with Jedidiah
Lapp. Did something happen?"

"Nee." Sarah shook her head. "We had a nice
time."

"But—" Josie invited.

Sarah sighed. "How well do you know the Zooks?"

"They are church members and friends. Why do
you ask?" Josie brushed her hands down her apron
before she reached up to tuck in a strand of hair that
had escaped from the rolled hair under her *kapp*.

Sarah didn't say anything at first. She didn't want
Josie to suspect how she felt about Jedidiah Lapp.

"I just wondered. We saw Annie Zook at Whittier's."

"Ah…" Josie flashed her a knowing smile. "You
heard that Jed and Annie were once thought to be
sweethearts."

Sarah bent down to hide her red face and check
all the plants for anything that was ready to be
picked.

"What?" Sarah said without looking up. "Were
they sweethearts?" she asked casually, as if she
wasn't eager to hear something that would prove
the thought wrong.

"He took her home from a singing a time or two."
Josie hunkered down to get back to work, and Sarah
felt relieved. "I think he liked Annie at first, but
once Noah married, Jed seemed to change."

"How?" Sarah kept her eyes focused on the task at hand, tugging gently on a stubborn weed near a bell-pepper plant.

"I don't know. I can't describe it." Josie started to pick green beans. "*Restless* might be a *gut* word for it."

Restless? Sarah thought. "How so?"

Josie shrugged. "It was as if he wanted more from life."

Sarah remained thoughtful as Josie began to talk of other things. She perked up when she heard Josie mention Rachel.

"I know Rachel has been wanting you to visit again," she said. "Why don't you go today after the midday meal?"

"But we have pies to bake for Sunday's visit," Sarah began, although she wanted to visit Rachel.

"We have the cakes you baked in the freezer that we can take. Besides, we have all of tomorrow to make pies if we want."

Sarah smiled. It was hard for her to forget about work and leave. She knew it was because she'd spent so many months handling everything for *Mam.*

"I'd like to visit her," she admitted. Josie looked up from weeding around a zucchini plant and grinned. *"Gut."* She went back to inspecting the small green squash that would soon be ready to pick. "This will be a *gut* year for zucchini."

Sarah nodded. "I imagine the garden back home is thriving. Who will pick and can the vegetables there?"

"Sarah," Josie said softly but firmly, "didn't you say that your family was being well cared for?"

Sarah met her cousin's gaze and nodded. "I did."

"Then the work will get done whether you are there or not. Isn't it better to enjoy what time you have here than to worry about the work at home?"

Sarah knew Josie was right, but old habits died hard. "I will try."

Her cousin's lips twitched with amusement. "That's all I shall ask of you."

After sharing a midday meal of egg-salad sandwiches complemented by sweet pickles and sweet-and-sour chowchow, Sarah wrapped up some lemon bars and chocolate brownies to take to the Noah Lapp cottage near the schoolhouse a mile down the road from the Mast farm.

"It's a lovely day for a walk," Sarah said before leaving.

"Why not take the buggy to the *schuulhaus?*" Josie suggested.

"I need it," William said as he entered the room. "I'm heading over to help Amos King fix a section of his barn roof."

"Don't you be falling off that roof, William

Mast," Josie scolded lovingly. "What of the young Lapp boys? Can't they fix it?"

"They're all busy today, and Amos says the barn has been leaking with every rainstorm. He's eager to get the work done."

Josie sighed. "Please be careful." She turned to Sarah. "You can take the courting buggy."

Sarah opened her mouth to refuse, but before she could utter a sound, William said, "I'll drop her by the cottage. I'll be going that way. It's just across the road from the Amos King farm."

Sarah smiled as she untied her apron strings. "I was going to say that it's a nice day for walking, but I'll take the ride and walk back."

"Gut." William nodded and Josie looked pleased. "I'll be leaving in five minutes. Can you be ready?"

"Ja. I'll just run upstairs and be right down." It would be better to take the ride to the cottage with the baked goods than to walk the distance.

As promised, Sarah ran upstairs to remove her cape and apron. She'd wear only her spring-green dress and white prayer *kapp.* On her feet she wore sneakers without stockings or socks.

She was outside next to the buggy when William joined her. He raised his eyebrows when he saw her seated in the buggy with the baked goods on her lap.

"I've never known a woman to be ready so quickly," he said with a smile.

Sarah simply smiled in return.

William was quiet as he steered the horse and buggy down the road toward the Lapp cottage. It was a pleasant silence between them. Sarah enjoyed the warmth of the summer day as well as the scenery that never failed to make her smile.

How did *Englischers* live in their fast-paced world? Did they ever stop to notice the wildflowers along the road, the tiny sprouts in the tilled fields that hinted at a good year's crops? Did they ever pause to smell the honeysuckle or take long walks just to breathe in the fresh air? Did they take notice of every little bit of life that the Lord generously gave them? God's wonders, she thought.

Sarah felt wonderful this day, as she did most days since coming to Happiness. She couldn't think of a better name for this village.

"William," she said, finally breaking the silence as they neared the Samuel Lapp farm and soon the Noah Lapp cottage. "I appreciate you having us— the twins and me. I know the boys can be a handful, and I don't doubt that it's harder to have all of us underfoot."

William drew up the leathers as they neared the dirt lane next to the schoolyard. He steered the horse onto the lane and then stopped to give her an incredulous look. "Sarah," he said, his tone gentle, "you are family. It has been *gut* having you here. You are welcome for as long as you like." He grinned. "You make the best cakes and pies, but don't tell Josie.

And the twins—they have been *gut* for Will and Elam. I've never seen them so happy." He clicked his tongue and spurred the horse on. "Josie loves having you, as well."

Sarah felt the sting of emotional tears. *"Danki,"* she said, murmuring the word they rarely spoke except on special occasions. They often showed with actions rather than with words their appreciation of someone's kindness.

William pulled up the horse near Rachel's cottage, and Sarah climbed out. "I will stop by when I leave to see if you want a ride home," he said.

Sarah smiled as she adjusted her *kapp*. "It is a nice day for a walk, but that will be fine."

As her cousin steered the buggy down the lane and then toward the Lapp farm, Sarah approached the cottage's front door and knocked. It was a few moments before Rachel opened the door. Her eyes looked red, as if she'd been crying.

"Sarah!" she exclaimed, happy to see her.

"Are *ya* all right?" Sarah asked as she stepped inside after Rachel opened the door wider for her to enter.

"I am fine," Rachel assured her. "I'm disappointed, but well."

"You're not going to have a baby," Sarah guessed. She set the plate she carried on top of a linen cabinet.

Rachel nodded. "I know I shouldn't feel this way,

but…" She drew a sharp breath. "I was so hopeful. I so want to have Noah's baby. He will make a *gut* father, and I feel like I've failed him."

Sarah placed her arm around the young woman's shoulders and led her to a kitchen chair. "It will be fine, Rachel. I feel it. The good Lord will provide." She sat down in another chair and leaned toward Rachel. "I will pray, Rachel. I feel He will give you the child you desire. You and Noah."

Rachel blinked back tears, sniffed and then smiled. "There is something about you, Sarah. You make me believe that God wants this for us."

Sarah nodded. "I believe it." She stood and looked toward the stove. "Can I make you a cup of tea?"

"I can do it." Rachel started to rise, but Sarah waved her to stay seated.

"*Ja,* but I'd like to make it."

"Then you may, certainly." Rachel wiped her eyes and then watched as Sarah made the tea, glancing toward her friend often as she worked.

"I brought lemon squares and chocolate brownies." Sarah went back to the linen chest and retrieved the dish she'd brought with her. She unwrapped the treats and set them on the kitchen table.

"You know us so well," Rachel said with a smile.

"I know you like lemon and Noah likes chocolate."

"I feel as if I've known you longer than just a few weeks."

Sarah understood. "I feel the same."

"I went to the doctor," Rachel admitted after they'd discussed simple things like the gardens, the weather and when school would begin again. "I drove myself."

"What did he say?" Sarah took a bite of a lemon square as she waited for Rachel to continue.

"That it is possible that I can conceive, but that it may be difficult."

"Then you will be carefully watched by a doctor when you do get pregnant."

"Ja." Rachel stood and took her cup to the sink. "I think Noah was disappointed."

Sarah shook her head. "Noah loves you. He would rather have you happy and healthy than have a baby." She smiled. "I've seen the way he looks at you."

"The same way that Jedidiah looks at you?"

Sarah felt a jolt. "He doesn't look at me that way."

An amused smile played about Rachel's lips. "If you say so." As if realizing that Sarah might feel uncomfortable discussing Jed, Rachel asked Sarah if she'd like to see the schoolhouse.

Sarah agreed. After they finished their tea, they walked over to the schoolhouse together.

Rachel pulled out a key and unlocked the door. "It seems so quiet with the children gone."

"But they will be back before you know it." Sarah enjoyed seeing all the wooden desks in rows that ran a few feet's distance from the teacher's station down the length of the room. She saw the alphabet and arithmetic charts on the wall. On each side of the door were two wooden cases with glass doors and books lining every shelf. Storybooks, Sarah suspected, as they didn't look like textbooks. When she relayed her thoughts to Rachel, she learned she was correct.

"The textbooks are in the bottom cabinet," Rachel said. "Those books are for the students to borrow and enjoy at home."

Sarah noted that the teacher's desk was particularly well made. When she commented on it, Rachel admitted that Noah had made it for her.

"He is a talented craftsman," Sarah said.

"The Lord gave him a wonderful gift," Rachel agreed.

They wandered about the classroom for a time, looking at some of the papers the students had written, the letters the younger ones had penned.

Rachel locked up the school when they were done, and they entered the yard to take a look at the swing sets. "The children enjoy them at recess," she said. She was quiet as she and Sarah walked back to the cottage. She paused near the cottage door. "Sarah, will you be staying the summer?"

"I don't know," Sarah admitted with a little pang. She was bothered by the fact that she'd be leaving soon. As much as she wanted to see her family, she wanted to stay here in Happiness.

"Will you write to me after you've gone home?" Rachel asked as she opened the door and they returned inside.

Sarah was touched. "I will be happy to." She bit her lip and then admitted, "I'll miss you and everyone in Happiness. This has become like home to me during the short time I've been here."

"Maybe one day you can come back for a visit," Rachel said.

"I'd like to." It all depended on *Mam*'s health and how much her family needed her.

How does *Jed look at me?* Sarah questioned later as she walked down the road, after a delightful afternoon spent with Rachel.

She liked Jed. The idea that he might like her as well thrilled her.

She'd never cared for a man like she cared for Jed, and she'd never had a man return her feelings.

Did she love Jed? *Ja, I love him,* she realized with a suddenly rapidly beating heart.

She thought of stopping at the Amos King farm to tell William that she was leaving, but she didn't want to bother him. *And what if Jed happens to be there?* Was she ready to see him so soon after coming to realize her love for him?

Sarah paused on the side of the street and closed her eyes. A car horn tooted, startling her, and she gasped. The weather remained lovely, and she looked around her. This was why she'd wanted to walk, wasn't it? To enjoy the wonders of God's work along the way?

Birds sang in the treetops. The scent of rose blossoms filled the air as she passed by a hearty bush. Children played on an *Englischer*'s lawn, laughing and running, and yelling, "You're it!" as they engaged in a game of "tag." A soft breeze blew across her skin, making her smile.

Life was beautiful. God had given them all wondrous things. God had given her Jed when she'd needed him most. She shouldn't worry about the future. She should trust in the Lord's love.

And she should protect her heart and keep her love for Jedidiah Lapp to herself.

Chapter Thirteen

Late Sunday morning, Sarah, the twins and the William Masts climbed into the family buggy and then headed toward the Samuel Lapp farm for a day of visiting. The day started out unusually warm. Sarah wore her lavender short-sleeved dress with white cape and apron. On her feet, she wore white sneakers. She'd washed her hair when she'd first risen at dawn, and after it had dried sufficiently, Sarah had rolled and pinned up the red-gold strands in the traditional Amish way. Then she'd covered her hair with the new white prayer *kapp* she'd made earlier in the week.

"Will," Timothy said from where he sat in the seat directly in front of hers, "do you think Jacob and Eli will play ball with us today?"

"If we ask them." Young Will, William's oldest son, grinned beneath his black-banded straw hat. "Someone will play with us."

"Maybe Jedidiah," Thomas said.

Sarah's heart skipped a beat at the mention of the one man she longed to see.

"He might," Elam said. "He's played with us before. Joshua King will play. So will David Schrock and Nate Peachy."

As the discussion continued around her, Sarah couldn't stop thinking about Jed. She'd always been comfortable with him. Should she allow the information Rachel had revealed change that? She knew she'd be watching him closely to see if she could see what Rachel had glimpsed—that Jed had feelings for her.

"Will there be a large group here today?" she asked conversationally, hoping to get her mind on other things.

Josie smiled as she glanced back to where Sarah sat in the farthest backseat. "Large enough. The Lapps have plenty of room."

"The Amos Kings, the Abram Peachys, the Eli Shrocks and the Joseph Zooks will be there," William said. "It will be a nice day for all."

"Ja," Sarah said, thinking of Jed and his promise to give her a tour of the farm.

Rachel and Noah had just arrived when William pulled their buggy into the yard near the farmhouse. Tables had already been set up outside. Children ran about the lawn, playing. A young girl with a rope about her waist pretended to be a horse while a boy held the two ends of the "reins" as they both ran among the others, who laughed and played and had fun.

Sarah was glad to see Rachel as she stepped from the buggy. She felt a feeling of warmth when she realized that her new friend was waiting for her.

"You look well today," Sarah said.

"I feel better than I did," Rachel admitted. "I appreciate your encouragement the other day."

"I didn't do anything." Sarah fell into step with Rachel, her arms cradling a basket of fresh-baked muffins and rolls. Josie and Ellen went ahead with the two pies and a chocolate cake that Sarah had made yesterday.

"*Ya* did a lot." Rachel placed a hand on Sarah's arm, halting their progress. "You reminded me how much Noah loves me and all the things I should be grateful for."

"What things?" Sarah said with a frown, then she laughed.

"I talked with him about it." Rachel paused. "You are right. He loves me. He said so from the first. He told me we could adopt if we couldn't…" Her voice trailed off as if it was too painful to actually say the words.

Sarah glanced back toward the buggies. "Here comes Noah now," she whispered.

Noah had stopped to talk briefly with William,

probably to ask him how the windows and doors were holding up, Sarah suspected.

Now he reached the two women and placed a hand gently on his wife's shoulder. "I enjoyed the brownies the other day, Sarah," he said with the boyish grin that she'd come to associate with him.

Sarah smiled. "I'm glad you liked them."

With his hand still touching Rachel, Noah leaned forward to take a sniff. "What's in the basket?"

"Not much," Sarah said. "Just some muffins, biscuits and rolls."

Noah grinned. "I like muffins, biscuits and rolls." He tried to take a peek. "Are any of them chocolate?"

Rachel chuckled. "Would you refuse a corn or blueberry muffin if it's all she brought?"

"*Nee.* I love them, too," he said.

Sarah exchanged grins with Rachel. "I just happen to have a dozen chocolate-chip muffins in here." She held up the basket.

Noah closed his eyes in gleeful anticipation. "May I have one now?"

"Noah!" Rachel scolded lovingly.

Sarah lifted the tea towel she'd placed over the basket of baked goods and allowed Noah to select a chocolate muffin.

His obvious delight was his thanks. "You are a *gut* friend to us, Sarah."

Katie Lapp came out of the farmhouse and headed in their direction.

"Hallo!" She smiled at her son and offered the same generous warmth to Rachel and Sarah.

Josie had disappeared inside to put the cake and pies out of the sun until they were ready to enjoy them later that afternoon.

Josie exited the house in time to see one of her sons running with a big stick in his hand. "Elam! Drop that stick. You'll fall on it and poke yourself."

Sarah heard a *"Ja, Mam"* in a subdued voice before the boy obeyed his mother, dropped the stick and rejoined the other boys.

"Boys," Sarah said with a smile.

"Ja," Katie agreed. "I've seen enough accidents to make you shudder. But now they know better. Even Joseph, my youngest, understands the danger of running with a stick. He's had his share of tumbles and accidents." Relieving Rachel from the burden of her casserole dish, Jed's mother gestured toward the house. "Come inside. Mae, Charlotte and Nancy are in the kitchen."

Rachel looked pleased. "Come, Sarah. I've introduced you to my aunt and cousins, haven't I?"

"Ja. I had the pleasure of meeting them at Sunday church services."

"I haven't seen them since," Rachel said. "I'm eager to talk with Charlotte."

As she followed Rachel and Katie inside the

house, Sarah recalled that Rachel had believed that Charlotte and Noah were sweet on each other at one time.

Her thoughts turned to Jed, and she turned to quickly search the yard for him. But he was nowhere to be found. She frowned. Where was he?

Jed heard the names Josie and William through the open window and he went to peer outside from his second-story room to look for Sarah. He knew she would be with them…unless she had gone home. *Nee,* she would have come to say goodbye, wouldn't she? They were friends, but in his mind, she meant more to him.

He found her standing with his sister-in-law Rachel and *Mam,* as if she enjoyed the women's company.

Should he head down now? She'd been on his mind a lot lately. He wanted her to keep company with him. He had promised to take her on a tour of the property—a good excuse to spend time alone with her, coupled with a genuine wish to show her their land.

He had enjoyed their day in town together. He'd loved watching her face light up as she'd eaten her ice cream, and had found it endearing the way she ate her lunch and later her bag of kettle corn.

The only awkward moment had been when they'd stopped at Whittier's Store for Sarah to call home.

He hadn't expected to see Annie there. They had chatted a bit—it was the polite thing to do—but his thoughts had been with Sarah and her phone call.

He had laughed at something Annie had said, but he couldn't remember what she'd said or why he had laughed. He'd wanted to wander the store with Sarah and Ellen. He'd wanted to stay near in case Sarah received bad news about her mother.

Eager to see her, Jed hurried down the stairs and headed toward the kitchen. He recognized her voice before he entered the room. He stood a moment, enjoying the soft, feminine lilt of her words as she talked with the community women, as they took care of the food. Eager to see her, Jed moved forward and made his presence known.

"It smells *gut* in here," he said as he joined the women.

"Jed!" Josie smiled as she gestured toward the desserts. "We have a lot to enjoy today."

"As we do every Sunday," he replied with a grin.

The other women greeted him, and then Jed made his way toward Sarah, who stood at the other end of the counter, placing rolls, biscuits and muffins from a basket onto a platter.

"*Hallo,* Sarah," he said softly, studying her fine hands as she worked, her profile, her beautiful red-gold hair pulled back and mostly hidden beneath her prayer *kapp.* He could see the delicate skin at her nape.

"Jed." She flashed him a quick smile before she continued the job at hand.

"May I show you around the farm later?" he asked, waiting eagerly for her answer.

"I'd like that," she said without looking up as she uncovered a bowl of potato salad and set a spoon into the potatoes.

Rachel approached. "What shall I carry?"

"The muffins and rolls?" Sarah suggested as she picked up the container of chocolate pudding. She glanced at Jed and held up the bowl. "The refrigerator?"

"In the back room." He smiled. "Follow me."

Sarah's gaze met Rachel's as the two women passed each other. Sarah saw amusement in her friend's expression, and she raised her eyebrows.

The refrigerator was in a back room next to a chest freezer. Jed opened the door, shifted a few things around and then held out a hand for the pudding bowl.

Sarah nodded her thanks, handed him the bowl and turned to leave.

"Sarah—"

The sound of his soft voice made her tingle. *"Ja?"* She didn't turn.

"Can *ya* eat dinner with me today?"

Sarah turned to him. "Josie…"

"I understand," he said softly, but there was a hint of something in his eyes. Disappointment? Longing?

She jerked with surprise. *Affection?* Could this be the look that Rachel had seen?

"But you can still show me around the farm," she murmured, suppressing the urge to touch her *kapp* to make sure her hair was neatly tucked inside.

She saw him study her, felt his interest in her as keenly as if he'd told her he liked her outright. She was suddenly conscious of her own feelings for him.

Nee, she thought. *I shouldn't do this. I'll be going home soon.*

Enjoy your time with him, her heart said. Tomorrow she might get that phone call or letter, making today their last day together.

"I'll see you later," she said quickly and then turned to hurry back into the kitchen—and the safety of the women's company.

Jed didn't follow her into the room. But when she went outside carrying items for the food table, she saw him seated at a table with his aunt and uncle and their five daughters. Jed spoke in earnest with his uncle, and Arlin seemed intent on whatever Jed was saying.

What were they discussing? Sarah wondered, and then she scolded herself for being so vain to think the topic of discussion was her. Vanity was a sin, and she knew the two men had more important things to discuss between them. *Lord,*

*help me to know what is right. Help me to be
strong, whatever happens.*

Jed sipped from a cup of coffee as he reached for
a muffin on the food table. He chose a cinnamon-
crunch muffin, and as he took a bite, he thought of
Sarah making it, with flour on her apron and a bit
of baking powder in her hair.

He would love to watch her bake. She was good
at it, and somehow he felt she'd look content as she
measured out the ingredients, stirred them in.

But it wasn't Sarah's baking skills that drew him
to her. It was her inherent sweetness. She'd sacri-
ficed much to take care of her mother, and did so
with love. Her concern for her family's welfare and
the welfare of others was a glimpse into what made
up Sarah.

He looked for her and saw her seated at a table
with her cousins. She was leaning close to Ellen
to listen carefully to what the young girl was saying. Sarah smiled and nodded as she straightened
in her seat.

Jed felt a tight feeling in his throat as he studied
her. He couldn't help himself; something drew him
to her. He didn't know if he'd be welcomed or not,
but he continued on.

His mother approached the other side of the table
from the opposite direction. Jed paused, wondering
if he should go on, but he kept going.

"Jed!" Katie Lapp said. "Would you mind help-ing your *dat* set up the badminton set?"

Jed saw the way Sarah went still as his mother mentioned his name. "*Ja, Mam.* Where is he?"

"On the back lawn."

He nodded. Before he left, he said, "Sarah, will *ya* be ready soon for that tour?"

She turned slowly, awarding him a glimpse of those bright blue eyes and sweet pink lips. But be-fore Sarah could answer, Katie said, "We'll be shar-ing midday meal soon, Jed. Why not wait until after we eat, when you can take your time showing her the farm and property?"

Sarah's blue eyes met his as he nodded. He saw an answer in her expression, and he saw agreement in her features…and a smile meant only for him. He felt his heart slam in his chest as he turned to leave. While he assisted his father, he thought of Sarah, the heady knowledge that he would be spending time with her soon. It seemed like ages ago when they'd gone into town, although it had only been a few days.

"Where did you get this?" he asked his father as they stretched out a net with a pole on each end.

"Rick Martin," Samuel said. "He dropped it by this morning. I would have put it away so that we could set it up for next Sunday, but Isaac and Dan-iel saw it and pleaded with me."

Jed grinned. "And so you had to put it up today."

"I think the Lord will forgive me this one little chore, don't *ya* think?" Samuel waved Isaac over and instructed him to hold one pole while Jed held the other. Next, he placed thin ropes about the top of each pole and grabbed the first of four stakes that would keep the poles standing up and balanced. Samuel extended his hand toward the ground for his hammer.

"*Dat,* let me," Jed said, grabbing the hammer. Samuel nodded and took Jed's position at one end of the net. Jed bent and quickly hammered two stakes at one end before securing the other two at Isaac's end.

"Can we play now?" Isaac asked when they were done.

"You can play now, but *Mam* may have other ideas. It's about time for dinner. You may play afterward," Samuel said.

Isaac looked disappointed for only a second. "I am hungry," he confessed.

"Didn't you have a biscuit or muffin?" Jed asked, lifting the boy's hat playfully before setting it back onto his head.

"That was two hours ago!" his brother said.

"Oh," Jed said with great understanding. "Then you definitely should get something to eat first."

Samuel and Jed exchanged amused looks as they walked back to the community area. Jed went into the barn and put away his *dat*'s hammer before returning in time to share in the meal that the Lord had blessed them with.

The deacon prayed over the food, and then the midday meal was shared in companionable enjoyment for all. Sarah, seated at the table with Josie, William and the children, rose to get her food. Josie and Ellen followed closely behind her.

As she picked up a plate and started down the food line, Sarah was startled when Josie said, "Sarah, you don't have to sit with us all the time."

Sarah looked at her. "Whom else would I sit with?"

"Rachel. Noah. *Jed*," her cousin suggested.

"Josie—"

"Jed will be taking you on a tour of the property, *ja?*" Josie speared a piece of cold fried chicken with a fork and placed it on her plate.

Sarah spooned a helping of potato salad. "*Ja,* Jed has offered to show me around." Why was her cousin bringing up Jed?

"Then why not sit with your friends? It's not every Sunday you can do so."

On church-service Sundays, the men ate together first, and when they were done the women and children sat down to eat their meal.

Visiting Sundays, at least, here in Happiness, Sarah noted, were more relaxed in their eating arrangements, as it was in her particular church community back home in Kent County, Delaware. Every church had its own set of rules. Their beliefs and teachings were the same, but as far as the way they dressed or the things they were allowed to do, the community's church elders decided those things.

"I told Jed that I'd be eating with you," Sarah admitted. She added some sweet-and-sour chow-chow to her plate.

Josie was silent for a moment. "I see."

Sarah flashed her a glance. "What do you see?"

Josie smiled. "You are worried about the twins again."

Sarah remained quiet. It was the first time that she hadn't thought of the twins, and she felt guilty for forgetting them in light of her feelings for Jed.

"They are fine with us." Josie chose a piece of frosted raisin bread.

"I know they are." Sarah chose a couple more food items, including a scoop of the green-bean salad and some dried-corn casserole. "I'm surprised at how well your two and the twins get along and behave together."

Josie laughed as she assisted her daughter Ellen with a helping of pasta salad that was just out of the young girl's reach. "I may have put the fear of God into them the first day they were here."

Sarah raised her eyebrows as she faced her. "How?"

"I told them that the Lord was everywhere, His

gaze especially on young, active boys who get into trouble. I said the Lord gives special blessings to those who are *gut,* do their chores well and play nicely with each other."

"And that worked?" Sarah was flabbergasted that so simple a warning had done so well.

"Well…" Josie grabbed a napkin and eating utensils before turning to head back to the table.

Sarah fell into step with her. Ellen had gone ahead.

"I hear a note of *but* in your tone," Sarah said before she sampled a sweet-and-sour cauliflower that was part of the chowchow mix.

"Actually, I told them that if they didn't behave, I'd send them over to help Jake Stoltzfus slog out his hog houses."

Sarah laughed. "The stench alone would be punishment enough for naughty boys. Would you have really sent them?"

"I am a woman of my word, Sarah. What do you think?"

Sarah was still chuckling as she sat down at the table while Josie and Ellen joined them. William flashed them a funny look, and Sarah could only grin at him. "Your wife makes me laugh" was all she told him.

William glanced at his wife, saw the amusement shimmering in her hazel eyes and said, "I don't want to know, do I?"

Josie smiled sweetly at him. *"Nee."*

Sarah became more acquainted with everyone who visited with the Samuel Lapps this day. The Eli Shrocks were Charlotte and Nancy's oldest sister, Sarah; her husband, Eli; and their children, David, John and Rose Ann.

Sarah had enjoyed a piece of coffee cake that Sarah King Shrock had made for dessert.

The Abram Peachy family consisted of the church deacon, Abram Peachy; his wife, Charlotte King Peachy; and the five Peachy children—Jonas, Nathaniel, Jacob, Mary Elizabeth and young Ruthie.

She saw the Joseph Zooks. She'd already met Annie and her sister Barbara. Horseshoe Joe and his wife, Miriam, had two sons as well—Josiah, who was older than Barbara but younger than Annie, and young Peter. She learned that the eldest Zook daughter had married and moved out of state.

She'd met Jed's uncle, Arlin Stoltzfus, in Delaware and since coming to Happiness, she'd became acquainted with his wife, Missy, and each of their five daughters.

"Sarah." Jed's deep voice coming from behind her startled her at first as it shivered along her spine. "Are you ready for the tour?"

Sarah rose from the table. *"Ja."* She picked up her paper plate and plastic utensils and put them in the garbage bag set outside for the day's event.

There was little to bring inside. Sarah looked

at the dessert table and wondered if she should carry something.

"I'll clean up," Josie said as she carried her own plate to dump into the trash bag next to Sarah.

"Are you sure?" As much as she wanted to go, Sarah was reluctant to run off without helping.

"Ja." Josie waved for her to leave. "There is little enough." She turned to smile at her daughter, who had come up behind them carrying not only her own plate but also several others from the table. "Ellen will help me with the desserts." The girl nodded.

Jed waited patiently, leaning against the massive trunk of a tree, not far from the Mast table. He pushed off at Sarah's approach. "I'll show you the house first, and then we can see the rest of the property from inside our buggy."

Chapter Fourteen

Jed gave Sarah a narrated tour of the farmhouse first. He took her through the first floor and gave his version of how the family utilized the space. Afterward, he led her up onto the second story, scooping up Hannah, who'd been napping in the first room and was now awake.

Sarah listened to Jed explain who slept where, while he carried Hannah comfortably in his arms. The way the little girl rested her head against Jed's shoulder as he walked told Sarah that Hannah had been picked up and held by Jed many times. It gave Sarah a warm feeling to see Jed holding his little sister so tenderly.

"This is where the twins and I sleep," Jed said, stopping before a door to a bedroom with four beds and a dresser. "Noah used to sleep here, too, before he got married."

Sarah looked quickly and then turned away, eager

to move on. Jed must have sensed her mood because he continued on.

"This room is where the youngest sleep—Daniel, Isaac and Joseph. That's *Mam* and *Dat*'s room across the hall. Hannah is the only one with her own room, and you saw how tiny it is. It's just big enough for her crib and when she is old enough, a twin bed." Jed stopped and smiled down at her, making Sarah's heart race and her stomach flip-flop.

"I like your home," she said, meaning it. The house looked well lived-in and loved. She could tell the Samuel Lapps were a loving family who cared about each other and their home.

Jed showed her Katie's sewing area—a small room off his parents' bedroom—and the upstairs bathroom before they headed down the stairs.

Sarah thought of her parents in their makeshift downstairs bedroom, and thoughts of her *mam* reached in and squeezed her heart. *She will get well,* Sarah had to remind herself.

"Shall we go outside?" Jed said. She looked up and saw him eyeing her with a concerned frown.

She smiled. *"Ja."*

"Are you interested in the barn?" he asked as he shifted Hannah to his other arm.

"Of course. An important part of any farm is its barn."

"And *Mam* has a greenhouse."

Sarah was eager to see it. "I remember. Does she have anything growing in it?"

"I'll show you after we tour the barn."

After setting Hannah down on his mother's lap, Jed took Sarah through the barn and saw how impressed she was with the building's cleanliness and the condition of the animals. Next he brought her to Katie's greenhouse. Inside were different plants in various stages of growth.

"I can understand why your *mudder* enjoys working in here." Sarah bent to examine an unfamiliar plant more closely. The label called it *Aloysia citrodora*.

"Lemon verbena," Jed explained. "It smells like lemons."

She leaned close to catch the scent. "You can make syrup out of it, can't you?"

"So I'm told. It's good over ice cream and probably other things, as well."

"And tea." Sarah took another whiff and then smiled. "I'm sure I've had tea made with lemon verbena." She looked about the greenhouse. "Katie has a large selection here, but I don't see any parsley or sage."

"Sold or given away," Jed explained. "Many of our church members come in the spring to purchase her herbs and seedlings, but *Mam* also gives a lot away—especially to family."

Sarah faced him with a smile playing about her lips. "I like your *mudder*. She is a kind and caring woman."

Jed grinned. "I like her, too."

Sarah chuckled. "I should hope so."

At Jed's invitation, Sarah preceded him out of Katie's greenhouse.

"I'll bring the buggy around. I think you'll enjoy a ride through our property."

Sarah nodded. She waved to Rachel and Noah, who approached. "Jed is going to take me for a ride through the property," she told them as they drew near.

"We'll go with you," Rachel said.

Noah gave her a wry smile. "*Mam*'s suggestion."

Jed brought the buggy around, and Rachel and Noah climbed into the backseat, while Jed helped Sarah into the front before joining her. If he felt bothered by his brother and sister-in-law's presence, Jed didn't show it.

The day was warm but not overly so as Jed steered the horse and buggy down the dirt driveway from the farmhouse to the main road ahead. He turned left onto the paved road and drove a distance before turning onto the road that ran past the school and cottage and continued down a length of Lapp property.

He stopped the buggy, climbed out and secured the horse to a small nearby tree. Noah got out the same side as Jed and helped Rachel out from the back. Jed skirted the buggy to assist Sarah.

"There is a stream just past that windbreak," Jed said, gesturing toward the line of trees to the right.

Noah and Rachel headed toward the trees, and as Sarah was about to follow them, Jed grabbed her hand and gently tugged her in another direction before releasing it. "I want to show you something."

His smile did odd things to her heart. The warmth of his fingers about her hand remained long after he'd released it. Sarah wished that he hadn't let go.

In silence, Jed led her farther down the dirt road. Sarah studied her surroundings as she followed his lead. To the left, corn grew in acres of farmland. To the right, the windbreak of trees had thinned. Sarah could see through the trees to farmland beyond. She wasn't sure, but it looked as if the field was filled with lush tall grass.

Jed stopped. With a light touch of her shoulder, he gestured toward the break in the trees. He started through the opening first, stopping as he reached the stream. Here the water width was so narrow they could easily jump across.

"Come," he said. He jumped over the water and then held out his hand to her.

Sarah looked at the stream and then his hand, and accepted his help. She felt the exact moment when his hand surrounded hers. This time he didn't let go. He laced his fingers with hers as they walked into the field, then paused. She studied the scenery before her and smiled. "It's beautiful here."

She glanced over in time to catch Jed's soft expression. "I bought this land from William and Josie. It once belonged to Josie's brother. He purchased it with the hope that he would build on it one day and bring a wife and family to live here."

He turned to eye the farmland, his brown eyes intent. "When he passed, Josie and her father came out from Indiana to see the land and decide what to do with it. It was during her time here that William and Josie met and fell in love."

"I didn't realize that Josie had lost her brother," she murmured, unable to break away from Jed's gaze.

"*Ja.* And she was heartbroken. She loved her brother, and it upset her that he never got to realize his dream."

"He never brought his wife?" Sarah finally looked away, her gaze returning to the land.

"He never married. He died in a farm accident in Indiana."

Sarah inhaled sharply. "How?"

"The horse attached to his plow spooked. He wasn't plowing the fields at the time. James's hands got caught in the reins. It happened so quickly that he couldn't get free."

Sarah closed her eyes, imagining the rest. James, she realized, had been dragged by his horse and caught under the plow. "I'm sorry." It had nothing to do with Jed, but she felt Josie and her family's pain.

"When Josie married William," Jed continued, "her family entrusted the land to the two of them. Later, when they decided to sell—especially since it was some distance from William's property— I asked if I could buy it from them. I had money saved from some construction work I did. I used it as a deposit and I continue to make payments. The land will be paid off next month."

Jed watched the play of emotion cross Sarah's face as he told her about the land and how he came to buy it. Did she have any idea what he was thinking?

He wanted a family and a home—with her. He knew her life was complicated and that he couldn't ask her to stay here and leave her family. But he had to let her know how he felt....

"Someday, I'm going to build a farmhouse on this land. I'll bring my wife here and together we'll raise our children."

Jed watched her closely as he spoke. He couldn't read her expression, and it bothered him. He had never told anyone about this land, certainly not Annie Zook. The only ones who knew were Josie and William, his parents and, more recently, his brother Noah, who was allowed to tell Rachel but no one else.

"The woman you marry will be happy here," she finally said. She released his hand to walk farther down the length of the field. "How far does it go?"

Disappointed in her reaction, he followed her. "It runs that way," he said, gesturing away from the main road by which they'd come, "to another road on the other side. The land starts here and goes there."

Sarah nodded politely. "So it starts here and heads away from the *schuulhaus.*"

"Ja."

She paused and turned to him with a smile that didn't quite reach her eyes. "I hope you and your wife will be happy here."

"Sarah—"

"We should go," she said, turning to head back the way they had come. "Rachel and Noah will be wondering where we've gone."

Jed felt a burning in his stomach as he nodded. "I wanted you to see this."

"It is beautiful. You will have a *gut* farm."

But not with you, Jed thought.

Surely she knew how he felt about her, but apparently her desire to go home was uppermost in her mind.

"Sarah—"

"Please, Jed. Don't!" she cried and hurried on, sprinting over the stream, through the trees and back onto the dirt road where the buggy lay ahead.

Jed followed slowly until he saw Noah and Rachel appear through the windbreak. He didn't want them to know what had happened. He needed to talk with Sarah, to make his love for her known, to see if there was a way for them to be together.

"It's wonderful here, isn't it?" Rachel gushed with a warm look at her husband. "The water is cool, but refreshing."

Sarah looked down and saw that her friend and Noah were carrying their shoes. "You went wading in the stream!" she exclaimed.

"A favorite pastime of ours," Noah said with an affectionate smile for his wife.

Sarah tried to chuckle, but her thoughts were in a whirl after learning of Jed's land and his future plans. Why was he telling her all this? Was he trying to let her know that after she went home, he and Annie were to be married?

She recalled the way their hands had entwined, how comfortable it felt to have him close, the warmth of his body radiating as he stood next to her.

Why did he bring her here? Because of Annie? She recalled Josie's claim that Jed had realized that Annie wasn't the one he wanted to marry.

Yet she recalled Jed deep in conversation with Annie…the laughter the two of them had shared while she'd looked on from a short distance away.

Soon she and the others got back into the wagon. She sneaked a quick peek at Jed, but she couldn't read his expression. She felt tension emanating from him, and she felt no comfort, no warmth that she'd felt before in his company.

She stared straight ahead as Jed continued to steer the buggy down the dirt road, which circled behind his father's farmland until they reached another dirt lane, which brought them onto the other paved road that Jed had mentioned. But instead of turning right to show her the land from the other side, he steered the horse left until he reached the lane that would take them back onto the farm and toward the farmhouse.

As Jed steered the buggy back into the barnyard, Sarah felt disappointed that the outing had come to an end. Something with Jed had changed during the ride.

He got out of the vehicle and then went around to her side. Extending a hand to her, he helped Sarah climb down. Silently, he started to turn.

She felt her stomach burn at the distance between them. "Jed—" she began.

He stopped and faced her, his expression unreadable.

"I enjoyed the day." She bit her lip, and it seemed as if he watched her closely. Noah and Rachel had left the vehicle and waited not far, but out of earshot.

"If I said something wrong," Sarah said, unable to control the tears that stung her eyes, "I'm sorry."

His expression softened. "You said nothing wrong, Sarah." He sighed. "The fault was mine."

Sarah frowned. "I don't understand."

"I thought you might like the land that I purchased—"

"I do!"

"And the fact that I plan to bring my future family there."

"It's a *gut* plan," Sarah said softly, trying hard to smile, but not succeeding.

"I thought so…"

Sarah hated this tension between them. "Jed, I'll be going home soon, and I don't want things to be bad between us." If he was with Annie, she couldn't ask him to write. The thought saddened her.

"That will never happen," he assured her, and she heard his sincerity. He studied her a moment. "I need to go see to Janey, our mare."

Sarah nodded. "The dessert has been brought out."

Jed glanced toward the tables set up in the yard. "I see that."

"Sarah," Rachel called to her, "are you coming?"

"Ja!" Sarah looked back toward Jed, but he was already moving away to park the buggy and take care of the horse.

She approached Rachel. Noah had gone ahead. "Where is Noah?"

"Abram Peachy asked to have a word with him."

Sarah followed the direction of Rachel's gaze as her friend glanced toward her husband. Noah was deep in conversation with the deacon and his wife, Charlotte, who was Rachel's cousin. Charlotte left moments later to join her mother at the food table.

"I have a feeling they have work for him," Rachel said with a smile. "While we wait for the men to join us, shall we head to the dessert table?"

"Ja." With a heavy heart, Sarah followed Rachel toward the food. While Rachel selected a couple of delicious-looking items for her and Noah, Sarah chose a piece of carrot cake for herself, and just in case Jed did return, she sliced him a good-size piece of the cherry pie.

Noah approached Rachel and Sarah a few minutes later. "You are the best wife," he told Rachel when he saw the desserts she had chosen for him. "I'm glad I married you."

"It's not hard to know what to get for you," Rachel replied. "As long as it's chocolate."

Sarah grinned as the two sparred teasingly before Noah actually sat and began eating the rich chocolate cake on the same plate as the chosen chocolate brownies and fudge.

Jed returned to find them as she continued to laugh at Noah, who heartily dived into the chocolate goodies. Sarah didn't have to look at Jed to feel his presence. She met his unreadable gaze before looking down to see the plate of cookies he'd brought.

He set the cookies down in the center of the table between them. "I brought these to share," he said directly to her.

Sarah felt a warmth spread through her belly as she slid the cherry pie across the table to him. "I thought you'd enjoy this."

His sudden grin warmed her heart and made her feel giddy inside. "Your cherry pie," he said before he dug into the flaky crust with a fork and brought a mouthful of the dessert to his lips.

"Your favorite," she murmured as she watched him enjoy his first bite.

"You are a keeper, Sarah."

His comment startled her.

"Perhaps you should marry her," Noah joked.

Jed's face suddenly became expressionless, and Sarah's spirits plummeted.

Rachel, immediately sizing up the situation, spoke up. "You say that to everyone," she told her husband teasingly.

"Can I help it if I want everyone to enjoy married life as I do?" Noah bit into a piece of fudge made warm and gooey from the day's heat.

"That's sweet of you, but you're embarrassing Sarah." Rachel smiled at her friend.

Sarah offered a half-hearted smile in return.

Sensing Jed's gaze on her, she flashed him a glance and saw a glimpse of something she couldn't identify, since it came and went so quickly. *Longing? Pain? Disappointment?* She couldn't tell.

The discussion turned to a different topic as Noah talked about the work Abram wanted done.

"While Charlotte was nearby, he asked for a new front door. After she left, he told me what he really wants—to surprise Charlotte with a rocking chair," he said.

"She'll love that," Rachel commented. "She appreciates quality furniture, and you always put a lot of time and care into everything you make."

Sarah took a sip from her glass of iced tea before setting it down. "I saw the desk you made for Rachel. It's lovely."

Noah frowned a moment before his brow cleared. "Ah, the teacher's desk," he said with a twinkle in his warm brown eyes.

"Well, she's the teacher, isn't she?" Jed said after happily swallowing a mouthful of cherry pie.

Noah bestowed a loving look on his wife. "That she is," he murmured, "and a *gut* one." He clearly enjoyed it when Rachel blushed.

The rest of the afternoon went by too quickly and soon Josie called out to Sarah, "We'll be leaving in a half hour."

"I'll be right there." Sarah stood. She should help to finish up in the kitchen. She mentioned it aloud.

"Nee," Rachel said. "We did what we could, and Katie and the others expect no more."

Sarah frowned. "But—"

"Sarah," Jed said softly, "you've done so much for so many months. Listen to Rachel. I'm sure Josie wants you to relax. In fact, I *know* she does."

Sarah felt warmed by Jed's tone and the way he looked at her.

"Jedidiah!" Timothy called as he ran toward them with Thomas fast on his heels. "Will you play ball with me?" The boy's gaze settled on Noah. "How about you, Noah? Will you play, too?"

Agreeing to play, the two Lapp brothers stood and followed the young Mast twins to the lawn, where Sarah saw other children waited to play, including the Peachy boys, David Shrock, Joshua and John King, and the younger Lapp brothers—Isaac, Daniel and Joseph.

Sarah watched them for a while, a smile on her face. She was pleased to see how good Jed was with the children. After a turn, she smiled at Rachel. "I should get up to help—"

"Nee. Jed is right, Sarah," Rachel said. "You've been working hard to help Josie. She told me so herself." She stood and picked up the empty plates. "You know that when you go home again, you'll be busy." She dropped them in a nearby trash can before returning to the table.

"It's hard to sit and not work—"

Rachel shrugged. "Enjoy it. It's Sunday and not a time for work. There is little to do. Let the others handle it."

They were silent as they watched the ball game in progress. Someone had brought out mitts and a bat. The game became a true baseball game with Jed pitching first and Noah in line to bat. Jed threw a pitch that had Noah swinging and grabbing only a little of the ball, which went careening off to the side.

"Foul ball!" Isaac Lapp shouted. He stood behind "home plate" as acting umpire.

Noah got ready for the next pitch. "Give it your best shot, *bruder,*" he taunted Jed.

Jed merely grinned and then pitched the ball. Noah swung, hit the ball hard, and sent it flying over the heads of John King and Timothy in the outfield.

Sarah laughed when she saw Jed shrug briefly as he looked her way.

"You like him," Rachel said, drawing her attention away from Jed.

"Who?" she asked but she knew what her friend was saying. She had realized only recently that her feelings for Jed had strengthened well beyond friendship.

Rachel's expression was knowing but warm. "Jedidiah."

Sarah frowned. "Rachel, please don't tell anyone."

"It's not my secret to tell," Rachel said with a

seriousness that reminded Sarah when Rachel had revealed a secret from her own past to her.

Sarah reached out to touch Rachel's hand briefly. *"Danki."*

I'm going to miss you when you leave." Rachel studied her with an intensity that spoke volumes.

"I'll miss you." Sarah swallowed against a suddenly tight throat. "I've been here longer than expected, but not long enough."

Rachel smiled as she reached for her iced tea. "The weeks have gone by too quickly." Her gaze went back to the boys playing baseball. "It's been *gut* for your *bruders* to be here." Jed shouted out encouragingly as a ball went sliding on the ground toward second base. "And you've been *gut* for Jed."

"I don't know about that," Sarah said, her eyes intent on the man she loved. "He's been nice to me because he knows I'll be leaving soon. I think he still cares for Annie Zook."

Rachel watched Jed closely before turning back to Sarah. *"Nee.* I know for a fact that he watches you when you're not looking."

Her friend had hinted at this before, but it was the first time Rachel seemed sure of the way Jed studied her.

Sarah glanced his way, but Jed was focused on the game. She turned back to Rachel. "He does?"

"Ja. All the time."

Sarah was surprised. She had caught him looking

at her in the past, but things had changed between them this week, ever since he'd taken her to Whittier's Store and encountered Annie Zook.

"Annie Zook didn't stay long today," Sarah said.

"*Nee,* her *grossmudder* is feeling poorly. She went home to stay with her." Rachel hesitated before continuing, "Her *grosselders* have had their share of trials this past year. Margaret Hershberger has been in and out of the hospital, and her husband has had a difficult time with his wife ill."

"Hershberger?"

Rachel's lips twitched. "You've met Alta Hershberger? She is Joe's sister-in-law. Joe and Miriam brought Miriam's parents to live in the *grosselders'* house when they moved to Happiness. They originally lived just north of Lancaster City. Joe's parents passed early on, so the house was ready and perfect for them."

"Barbara, Josiah and Peter are still here," Sarah noted. The three were Annie's siblings.

"Annie, Barbara and Miriam take turns caring for Miriam's *mudder.* It's a *gut* arrangement and seems to work out well."

Except Annie had to leave while Jedidiah remained behind.

"Does Jedidiah truly watch me when I'm not looking?" Sarah asked, loving the thought.

Rachel nodded. "*Ja,* he does."

Sarah recalled the way Jed had held her hand long

after he'd helped her cross the stream. She felt confused. Jed was a sincere, kind person; he wouldn't have held her hand if he didn't like her.

But liking isn't the same as loving.

Chapter Fifteen

Sarah moved about the worktable, cleaning up after a morning of baking. The scent of homemade bread and chocolate-chip cookie bars filled the kitchen, tempting one to take a sample.

Josie wiped the table while Sarah washed bowls, utensils and pans. "I can't wait to try the cookie bars."

"I'm wanting a taste of bread with a pat of butter." Sarah rinsed off a soapy bowl and placed it in the dish drainer. She washed out a bread pan next. Three loaves sat on cooling racks on the counter. She dipped the pan into the sudsy water and used a pad to scrub off the residue left by the baked bread.

When she was done cleaning their workspace, Josie grabbed a towel and began to dry the dishes Sarah had washed. "The boys loved those cherries you brought back from town last week."

Sarah shot her a wry look. "I had planned to

make a couple of chocolate cherry pies with them—
one or two for the family and one for Jed. I wanted
to show my appreciation for taking me into town."

Josie grabbed the newly rinsed bread pan. "You
bought the cherries with your money," she scolded.

"*Ja,* of course. This was to be my gift to you and
William…and Jed."

"I'll give you the money to buy more—" Josie
began.

"*Nee.*" Sarah washed the last of the dishes and
emptied the plastic sink basin. "You all enjoyed
the cherries, didn't *ya?*" Josie agreed that they had.
"Then the cherries were as *gut* as the pie."

"Except that Jed didn't get any."

Sarah shrugged. "I've given him a pie before. I'll
think of something else to make him."

A car horn beeped outside. Sarah and Josie
looked out the window just as a black SUV pulled
into the yard and came to a stop not far from the
farmhouse.

"Who is that?" Sarah asked.

Josie hurried to the door with dish towel in hand.
"Let's go find out."

Sarah followed behind Josie as she stepped out
onto the front covered porch and waited for the oc-
cupants of the vehicle to alight. A young Amish
man stepped out first and then reached in to help
a woman out.

"Oh, my!" Sarah gasped. "It's Emma!" The

woman was her older sister, Emma, the man Emma's husband, James. It had been over a year since she'd seen the Yoders. She ran to her sister and grabbed her hands. "'Tis wonderful to see you!" Emma pulled her into a quick hug. "What are you doing here?" Sarah frowned. "Is it *Mam?* She's taken a turn for the worse! You've come to take us home!" Her stomach clenched with terror.

"*Nee,* Sissy, *nee,*" Emma said, grabbing her by the shoulders and giving them a squeeze. She gave Sarah a warm smile. "*Mam* is fine. She is mending nicely. She has weeks of recuperation yet, but the doctor expects her to make a full recovery."

Sarah closed her eyes and prayed. "Thanks be to God." She opened her eyes to see James taking a suitcase out of the hired car. "You're staying?"

"*Ja.* Josie was nice enough to invite us." Emma turned to grin at her husband as he carried their suitcase toward them.

"How did you know where we were? Why have you come? How do you know that *Mam* is well? How long will you stay?"

"I knew you were here because *Dat* told me. I know that *Mam* is well because I asked *Dat.*" Emma smiled at Josie, who didn't look surprised to see her, Sarah noted. "And I'm here to see you and the twins."

As if mentioning them called them by name, the twins, followed by Josie's two young sons, burst out of the house and headed toward the barn. Timothy grabbed Elam's hat and started to run; the others gave chase.

"Boys!" Sarah cried.

Thomas stopped without turning. "*Ja*, Sissy?"

"Come say *hallo* to your sister."

"Emma?" Thomas saw his eldest sister and let out a whoop. "Timothy! Emma is here." He saw her husband beside her. "And James!"

Timothy, who'd been laughing and holding Elam's hat out of reach, paused and without thinking lowered his arm.

Elam quickly grabbed his hat and placed it back on his head. He scowled at Timothy. "Who is Emma?" he said, as if he'd just noticed Timothy's expression.

"My sister," the twin whispered. "Emma?" he said more loudly. He approached and saw that the dark-auburn-haired woman was indeed his eldest sister.

Emma gave him a scolding look. "What were you doing with that hat?"

Timothy dropped his eyes as he came closer. "We were just playing."

Elam and Will followed behind Timothy, curious to see what was going on.

"*Ja*," Elam said, as if he realized that his cousin Timothy might be in trouble. "We were just playing."

Emma eyed the boys sternly for a minute before

she grinned and extended her arms. "Well? Aren't *ya* going to give your big sister a hug?"

Timothy nodded happily and then ran into Emma's arms. Emma looked at Thomas over Timothy's head. "What about you? Too big for a hug?" Holding Timothy with one arm, she extended the other to his brother. Thomas shook his head, grinned and ran in for a hug. "You're getting so big! What happened to my baby brothers? You're growing up too fast!"

"Ja," Thomas said proudly as his eldest sister released them. *"Dat* measured us last month. We growed an inch!"

Emma studied him seriously. "I can see that. It looks like you grew a foot since I last saw you." She addressed Josie: "We appreciate the invitation."

"My pleasure." Josie waved the boys to go back to their play. "I thought your sister might enjoy the visit."

Sarah flashed Josie a wide-eyed glance. "You knew she was coming?"

"Ja. I wrote and invited her." Josie wiped her hands on the kitchen towel. "I'm happy that you came," she said to Emma and James.

"And the timing was *gut,"* James said as he set down the suitcase and straightened.

"We are pleased that we could both come," Emma said with a loving look at James.

"I'm stunned," Sarah admitted. Now that she

knew *Mam* was fine, she was excited to be able to spend time with her sister. She had missed Emma since her sister had married and moved to Ohio. "How long will be you be staying?"

"A few days," James said. "I can't stay away from the farm much longer."

"Come inside," Josie invited.

Sarah followed her family into the house. Her thoughts went to Jed, as they often did during the day and every day since she'd first seen him. She wondered if she'd get to see him again soon and what her sister would think of the kind, young man to whom she had lost her heart.

"Sarah's sister has come to visit." Rachel moved about the cottage's kitchen, making lunch for Noah and Jed, who was helping his brother at the shop this day.

"Sarah has a sister?" Noah asked. "I thought she only had brothers."

"*Ja,* she has one older sister," Jed said, revealing the fact that he knew a great deal about the red-haired girl. "Emma. She lives in Ohio with her husband—James, I think his name is."

Rachel looked at him knowingly. "It is James."

"Is she glad to see her?" Jed raised a glass of iced tea to his lips.

"*Ja,* it's been over a year since she's seen Emma."

Rachel set a sandwich plate before each man. "I'm sure she's missed her."

"I can only imagine what Sarah must have thought when Emma arrived. With her mother recovering from surgery, she must have thought her *mam* had taken a turn for the worse."

Rachel nodded. "I stopped by yesterday and that's exactly what Sarah told me."

Jed felt a tingling warmth as Rachel spoke of Sarah. Poor Sarah! How worried she must have been!

It had been three days and forty-five minutes since he'd last seen her. He missed her like a flower missed the sunshine. He had kept his distance intentionally. Did she miss him? When he'd showed her his property and told her of his plans, she'd seemed a bit cool, unaffected, and he'd been hurt. These past days he'd thought that by staying away he'd get over her, but he was proved wrong.

Sarah Mast was constantly in his mind from the time he woke up in the morning until bedtime, and during the night he often dreamed of her: her lovely face smiling as she stood next to him by the stream that bordered his new property, on the front porch of a new farmhouse cradling an infant—their infant—in her arms.

"Do the sisters look alike?" Noah asked after chewing and swallowing a bite of roast-beef sandwich on homemade German rye bread.

"There is some resemblance. Emma's eyes are green. Emma's hair is a dark red, while Sarah's—"

"Is red kissed golden by the sun," Jed finished. He averted his gaze from Noah's knowing glance.

"So when are you going to meet her sister?" Noah asked.

Jed hesitated for only a second. "After we're done at the shop." His brother was a skilled cabinetmaker who created furniture to order. Noah had needed a little help to get caught up on a few orders. They'd accomplished a lot that morning, but there was more work to be done.

"You've worked enough today." Noah took a sip of lemonade. "In case you'd like to visit after lunch."

"I can work a little longer." Jed grabbed a cookie and took a bite.

"*Nee,* brother," Noah said. "You'd better get over to the Masts' this afternoon. It's the best thing to do, for all of us."

"Why?" Jed bit into a cookie.

"Because we're tired of seeing your unhappy face, that's why," Noah said. "And the Lord wants you to visit her."

Jed frowned. "How do you know?"

"Because I've seen how you are with her. Any woman who makes you happy whenever you're with her is a gift from God. We should always accept what the Lord wants for us."

"Is that how you felt about Rachel?" he asked,

turning to study his sister-in-law, who came out of a back room.

"*Ja,* it's exactly how I felt."

Jed pushed back his chair and stood. He grabbed his straw hat from a wall hook and set it on his head. "Lunch was *gut,*" he told Rachel with a smile. Then he turned to his brother. "And so was the advice."

Jed hurried home to clean up before heading out to the William Mast farm to visit Sarah.

Seated at the kitchen table with Emma and Josie, Sarah heard the clip-clop of horse hooves on dirt and the sound of turning buggy wheels in the yard.

"William must be back from Abram's." Josie set a cup of tea before Sarah's sister.

"That was fast." Sarah gratefully accepted a cup for herself. "I thought he had a full day's work there."

Josie shrugged. "They must have finished sooner than they thought."

Emma bit into a cinnamon-streusel muffin. "These are delicious, Josie."

"Sarah made them." Josie pulled the platter of muffins closer and selected one to put on her own plate.

"Sarah did?" Emma studied her sister.

"*Ja.* She's been doing all the baking since she's come."

"You're a *gut* baker, Sarah." Emma took another bite.

"She's a *gut* cook, too," Josie said. "She's been a blessing to us all. It's been wonderful having her here."

Footsteps resounded on the front porch. "Jedidiah!" Sarah heard Timothy exclaim. Josie's boys and Thomas echoed Timothy's greeting. "You want to play ball?"

She heard the rumble of Jed's familiar deep voice in answer. "Not today, but we can play another day." She heard the agreement among the children and then the sound of a knock on the door.

Her heart started to pound. Jed was here? It had been days since she'd seen him, since the awkwardness had happened between them after he'd taken her on the tour of his family's farm and told her about his plans with Annie as he'd shown her his property.

Had he expected her to be happy about his relationship with Annie? When she loved him herself? *But he doesn't know I love him.*

Sarah rose and went onto the porch. "*Hallo,* Jed." He looked wonderful, she thought with a pang of longing.

"Sarah! How are you? I've come to visit you." He smiled and stepped up onto the porch to stand next to her. "I've missed you," he said softly.

She stared at him, startled by his admission. "I've missed you, too."

His grin did odd things to her. "Do you have time for a walk? If you're not too busy…"

Sarah wanted nothing more than to walk with him. "My—"

"Hallo." Emma had stepped outside and was eyeing Jed curiously. "You must be Jedidiah Lapp. I've heard a lot about you."

"From who?" Sarah frowned. She hadn't told her sister about Jed.

"Mam and *Dat.* Who else?" Emma smiled at the man Sarah loved. "You rescued my brothers."

"'Twas nothing—"

"It was definitely something," Sarah insisted. She was surprised to see him blush. "Jed, in case you haven't figured it out—this is my sister, Emma."

Emma came closer and smiled. "Nice to meet *ya,* Jed."

"Gut to meet you, too." He studied her sister. "You look a lot like your *mudder,"* he said.

"So I've been told." Emma glanced back as Josie exited the house.

Looking distracted at first, Josie smiled and the frown on her brow cleared. "Oh, *hallo,* Jed. How's your *mudder?"*

"She's well. She wanted me to remind you about the quilting bee tomorrow. She's sorry she had to cancel it for today, but Joseph has a doctor's appointment she'd nearly forgotten."

"Tomorrow is better for me anyway."

"Sarah and I are going for a walk. Would you care to join us?"

Sarah sent her sister a look. "*Nee,* but it was nice of you to ask," Emma said. "I've got laundry to do, and I promised to help Josie with her mending."

Sarah was relieved. It wasn't that she didn't want to spend time with her sister, but she didn't know how much longer she would be in Happiness, and she wanted to spend as much time as she could with Jed—alone.

Josie looked off in the distance toward the pasture. "If you're heading toward the back fields, would you tell William and James that we're holding their lunch for them?"

"*Ja,* of course," Sarah said. She looked to Jed.

Jed agreed, "We'll find them."

Emma and Josie returned inside, and after a quick greeting, the boys had returned to the barn where they'd been grooming the horses.

"Are you ready to go?" Jed asked softly.

Sarah nodded and fell into step beside him as they walked past the barn and into a farm field.

Chapter Sixteen

They walked in silence for a time. The day was hot, but not uncomfortable. Birds chirped in the nearby trees. A bee buzzed in a honeysuckle bush. A soft breeze tousled the bushes and leaves and even the grass that carpeted the surrounding area of the house and barn.

Sarah could feel Jed's presence keenly. The warmth of his nearness, his clean masculine scent, made her overly aware of his movements beside her.

"I should have been by sooner." Jed stopped and faced her. "I was upset the other day—"

"Jed." She put her hand on his arm, feeling the muscle, and then quickly released it. "I'm not certain what happened, but something changed between us during our tour of the property."

Jed inclined his head. His expression was somber. Sarah loved everything about him: his dark hair beneath his straw hat, the way his cinnamon-brown eyes studied her. He wore a royal-blue shirt and dark blue tri-blend denim pants with black shoes. She couldn't help noticing the way his shirt fit him under his black suspenders.

"I'm sorry about that day, Sarah. I wasn't in the best mood, and I don't want anything to ruin our friendship."

"I don't want anything to ruin it, either," Sarah breathed.

Jed grinned. *"Gut."* He gestured ahead. "Let's tell William that Josie is waiting for him at the house, and then we'll go back and head in the opposite direction."

Sarah enjoyed her walk with Jed. They chatted about many things, including the sale at Spence's Bazaar in Dover, Delaware, and the Plain and Fancy restaurant in Bird-in-Hand that offered delicious family-style food to the locals and tourists.

"'Tis *gut* to spend time with you," he said as they changed direction toward the north pasture, where William and James examined one of William's cows.

"I've enjoyed it, too." She hesitated. "I wasn't sure I'd see you before I left."

"You're going home?" He studied her with a frown.

"I don't know. Emma said that *Mam* is doing well and everyone at home is well taken care of."

She was pleased when she sensed him relax. "*Gut.* Then maybe you'll get to stay longer."

"Maybe." She gave him a slight smile. She quickly changed the subject, because the thought of leaving upset her. "So now you have met my sister."

"*Ja.* You have the look of sisters between you." Jed waved at William, who had caught sight of them. He then turned to grin at her. "You may have a family resemblance, but I find I favor golden-red hair and blue eyes."

Sarah's cheeks bloomed bright red. Her cousin and brother-in-law were just up ahead. "William! James!" she called as they approached the two men.

"*Hallo!*" William rose from his hunkered-down position near the animal. "Jed, what brings you out this day?"

"'It's been a while since I visited." Jed flashed Sarah a glance, and her face grew warm again.

"Josie's been keeping lunch for you and James," Sarah told William, enjoying the knowledge that Jed had come to the farm to see her. She was so caught up in Jed's presence that she nearly forgot to introduce him to James.

"James, this is Jedidiah Lapp. Jed, this is my *bruder*-in-law, James Yoder."

The two men greeted each other. Each appeared to size up the other and apparently liked what each saw.

"So, you're the one I've been hearing so much about." James took off his hat to wipe the perspiration from his forehead. A short sandy-brown beard edged his jaw, a testament to his newlywed status. "From Emma's parents. We visited there before we came here."

Sarah was stunned. "Emma didn't tell me you went to see *Mam*."

"*Ja,* well, we were only there two days—just until we could see for ourselves how she and the family are managing."

"And?" Sarah narrowed her gaze as she studied her brother-in-law.

"They are doing well. We haven't seen *Mam* for over a year—since the time we last saw you." James set his hat back on his head and readjusted it. "Emma was eager to see her."

Sarah frowned. "But she's well?"

"*Ja.* According to Iva, Ruth has her color back. She's moving slowly, as she should, but she has more energy and she smiles often. She's able to breathe more easily."

Sarah relaxed. She needed to have a discussion with her older sister. She and Jed exchanged glances. "Shall we tell Josie that you're on your way?"

"*Nee.* We'll head back now." William turned to James and gestured toward his animal. "So what do you think?"

"She looks fine to me," James said. "Whatever bothered her previously seems to have resolved itself."

James, Sarah knew, had a herd of dairy cows. He was knowledgeable regarding the animals, and William must have sought James's opinion on this one.

William ran his hand along the cow's back. "Let's go," he said to James. "Have you eaten?" he asked Jed and Sarah. Both nodded.

William and James accompanied Sarah and Jed back to the farmhouse.

As they neared the barn, they heard a loud cry. "Help!"

Jed looked and saw one of the twins hanging from the barn-loft window, barely able to hold on. "Dear Lord, please help him," he heard Sarah gasp.

Seeing the danger, he reacted immediately. "Stay below in case he falls," he called out to James and William, who looked for something to catch him in the event the boy fell. He ran into the barn. Spying the ladder, he hurried up the rungs and urged Timothy away from the loft window and his twin brother, who was barely able to hang on.

"Help!" Thomas cried but only weakly. "I'm… losing…my…grip!"

Jed approached carefully, quickly sizing up the situation from above. "Thomas, you trust me, don't you?" He saw it in the boy's eyes as he met Jed's gaze. "I'm going to grab hold of your hands and pull you up. Don't panic, all right?"

"*Ja.*" It was barely a whisper.

Praying silently, Jed reached down to grab hold of the boy's wrists, which wasn't easy, since Thomas dangled by his fingers. *Please, Lord, help me to save Thomas!* He made a grab for the boy's wrists and tugged hard, wincing when he heard the scrape of body against wood as he pulled Thomas up and into the loft. With his heart beating wildly, Jed hugged the trembling boy hard before he picked him up and brought him to the top of the ladder.

At the bottom, Sarah looked frightened. "Thanks be to God!" she cried as she examined her brother, who stood within Jed's arms, before she met the gaze of the man she loved.

"Sarah, can you climb up and help Thomas down from below?" Jed said. "I'll be above ready to catch him if he starts to fall."

She nodded. "Thomas, listen to whatever Jed says."

"*Ja,* Sissy," her brother said weakly.

Jed turned to Timothy behind him. "Can you climb down by yourself?"

Timothy gave a nod. "I can do it."

"*Gut* boy!" Jed applauded him. He released Thomas and helped the still-shaking boy onto the ladder rungs. "I'll be right above you. I won't let you fall."

With Jed's watchful encouragement from above and Sarah's position below as the boy climbed down, Thomas was soon on the ground, where he began to cry. Sarah reached out to hold him, her face crumbling at her brother's obvious fear and remorse. He could tell that any urge to scold him had promptly died as Thomas cried.

William had run inside the house for a blanket, and soon Josie, Ellen and Emma were outside watching Jed's rescue of Thomas from below. They each had hold of a blanket edge, ready to catch the boy should he fall.

With her arm about Thomas, Sarah watched as Timothy climbed easily down the ladder. When both boys were safe, she released her traumatized brother, who ran to his older sister, Emma.

Sarah approached Jed, who studied the Mast family as they rejoiced over the little boy's safety. "Jed?" she said softly as she drew near. "It seems like you are always there to rescue my *bruders.*" She met his gaze, her blue eyes bright with tears. Jed caught his breath at what he saw in the depths of her glistening blue orbs. She touched his arm. *"Danki."*

He swallowed hard. "I'm glad I was here to help."

"I don't know what I will do without you when we go home."

Jed glanced down at her hand. Her touch felt warm and wonderful on his biceps. *I don't know what I will do without you, either,* he wanted to say, but he kept silent instead. This wasn't the time or place to be having a discussion of his feelings for her.

The others entered the farmhouse, including the twins and Will and Elam, who had been upstairs in their bedroom. They'd hadn't known about Thomas's near-accident until they'd heard the commotion outside the same time as their mother had.

Jed stayed outside with Sarah. He had suggested a walk in the other direction earlier, but now it was too late and he had to return home to help his father. "Sarah, I have to go. May I visit another day?"

Sarah inclined her head. "*Ja.* I'd like that. It was *gut* of you to come—"

"I wanted to," he replied, and he saw her expression soften. "I wish I could stay longer."

He felt warm inside. He loved her smile, the way her vivid blue gaze regarded him with understanding and gratitude. There was something about her that made him want to stay and just stare at her all day long.

"I need to talk with Emma." Her smile turned wry. "She never told me that she visited *Mam*—"

"Hmm." Jed was thoughtful. "I wouldn't be upset with her. She may have decided you'd worry more if she told you of her fears. I can understand that she had to see for herself how your mother was recovering."

"But she could have told me she'd gone—"

Jed placed a hand on her shoulder. The warmth of her reached up to tug at his heart. If he wasn't careful, he might say something he wasn't quite ready to say and she wasn't ready to hear. He quickly released her.

"Sarah," he began softly, "you've been there for your *mudder* since she became ill. Emma was miles away with her new husband. You told me yourself that Ruth didn't want Emma to worry about the twins, since she was newly married. I'm sure she didn't tell her how ill she was, either, until she had the surgery and then someone was forced to tell her."

Silent, Sarah stared off into the yard. "I would be upset if *Mam* had kept her illness from me." She met his gaze, her expression serene. "I didn't think of this."

"Talk with Emma."

She nodded. "I will."

"*Gut.* I will see you tomorrow at the house." He wanted to capture her hand, give it a squeeze, but he wouldn't. The last time he'd held hands with her he'd told her about his dreams to marry and build a home. When she looked at him in question, he said, "The quilting bee *Mam* is hosting?"

"*Ja, ja,* of course."

"I will see you soon, Sarah." He gave in to the urge to briefly touch her cheek.

"*Gut* day to you, Jedidiah," she murmured.

Jed climbed into his buggy, took up the reins and urged the horse to move. He glanced back over his shoulder several times and was happy to note that she continued to watch him as he drove the buggy down the lane toward the main road.

Chapter Seventeen

The next day, Sarah and Emma, along with Josie and the four young boys, who tagged along with them, went to the quilting bee at Katie Lapp's. As soon as they arrived at the Samuel Lapp farmhouse, the children ran to find Jed's youngest brothers—Daniel, Isaac and Joseph—while the women went inside.

"Hallo," Katie greeted them with a warm smile. "I see you brought a cake."

"Sarah made it," Josie said, holding up the plate.

Sarah, who was looking about for a glimpse of Jed, heard her name and smiled at her hostess. "I enjoy baking," she said.

"You'll make some lucky man a *gut* wife someday." Katie accepted the cake from Josie and gestured for the women to enter the great room.

"I'm afraid I wasn't able to bring down the quilting frame. My sons were busy this morning, but some have returned. I'll see that they set it up for us."

"Can I help?" Sarah asked.

"*Nee,* but I appreciate the offer. It's a bit cumbersome. Jacob and Eli will take care of it for us. They've done it before."

Where is Jed? Sarah wondered. He'd told her he'd see her here today.

Jacob and Eli entered the great room and greeted the women. "You must be Sarah's sister," Jacob said.

Emma nodded. "It's nice to meet you."

"Jed said that he met you." Jacob studied Emma and then compared her to her sister. "*Hallo,* Sarah."

Sarah smiled. "Jacob," she greeted. "Eli."

Katie came out of the kitchen with a pitcher of iced tea. "Jacob, Eli, would you set up the quilting frame for us?"

"*Ja, Mam,*" Eli said and Jacob agreed. They apparently knew where to find it, as they immediately left the room and Sarah could hear their footsteps as they climbed the stairs to the second floor.

Emma watched as the young men left. "How many sons do you have?"

"Seven. Seven sons and one daughter."

"*Seven sons?*"

Sarah saw Katie smile at her sister's startled look.

"*Ja.* Jacob and Eli are third-born." Katie grinned. "Actually, third-and fourth-born but on the same day."

"They're twins, Emma," Sarah said with a chuckle.

"Fraternal twins." Jacob's hair was dark brown; he looked a lot like his older brother Jedidiah. Eli was fair-haired, and he had his mother's eyes and her warm smile.

Rachel entered the room and greeted everyone. "Where is Jed?" she asked Katie conversationally after a quick knowing look at Sarah.

"He had to work today. A local company called him for a new construction job. It was unexpected. Samuel didn't need him on the farm today, so Jed went."

Sarah's excited anticipation of seeing Jed again dissipated. "Does he like the work?" Emma asked.

Curious herself, Sarah waited for Katie's reply. "*Ja,* he doesn't mind it. Jed is a hard worker. Like his *vadder* and *grossdaddi,* he is *gut* with his hands. Samuel's *dat* was a cabinetmaker, although his age has slowed him down."

"Noah learned woodworking from his *grossdaddi,*" Rachel said.

"*Ja,* Noah's furniture shop is doing well." Katie set the pitcher of tea on a table near clean glasses and a plate of baked goods. "Samuel's *vadder* helps out Noah if he is feeling well enough. And Jed works at the shop from time to time, whenever Noah needs an extra hand."

Jacob and Eli returned, carrying lengths of one-by-three boards, which they promptly laid out on the floor to form a square. Katie exited the room for a moment and returned with a neat stack of the quilt squares hand-sewn by the community women. "I stitched them together with my sewing machine. Rachel, would you get the rest of the quilting material from my sewing room?"

Rachel agreed, and Sarah asked, "Can I help?" Her friend nodded. Sarah followed Rachel upstairs to Katie's sewing room, where they found a large piece of fabric to be used for the quilt backing, created by sewing together three lengths of the same material. Several bags of batting lay on a table next to Katie's treadle sewing machine.

Rachel picked up the fabric. "Can you manage the batting?"

"*Ja,* I've got it." Sarah balanced all the bags in her arms and followed Rachel down the steps.

The two women returned to the great room to find that many other community women had arrived and were discussing their families, the day and the quilt they would be stitching.

Jacob and Eli helped Rachel and Sarah set up the backing, batting and top layer of quilt squares stitched together by Katie. They stretched the quilt-to-be over the rack and pinned each layer into place on each length of the four boards secured together with C-clamps. Soon the women were seated around the quilting rack, talking and laughing and telling tales.

Later, on the way home, Emma expressed her

enjoyment of the day. "The Lapps are a wonderful family."

"Ja," Josie said, "and they are *gut* neighbors and friends."

"Their little Hannah is a darling," Emma commented softly as she gazed out the buggy window opening.

Sarah smiled, recalling how Jed's little sister, Hannah, had walked up to Rachel and held out her arms to be picked up. Rachel had immediately obliged by lifting the child onto her lap and cuddling her.

"I don't know when I last went to a quilting bee," Emma admitted softly. "Back home, in Delaware, it was. I wonder if any of the women near Millersburg would be interested in working together on a quilt."

"I'm sure they will. Some of the women may get together already to quilt once a week or month."

"Ja," Emma said. "I supposed that's true." She was quiet for a time until they arrived home and entered the house. "Sarah, we'll be leaving tomorrow. Would you help the boys pack their things?"

Sarah felt a clenching in her stomach. *"Ja."* She headed upstairs with an overwhelming feeling of sadness. The time had finally come to head home. Should she look for Jed and tell him she'd be leaving? Then she recalled what Katie had said about Jed working the new construction job. He'd be on-site long hours for the next few days. How could she say goodbye without disturbing his sleep? Should she leave him a note?

She couldn't see herself leaving a quickly penned note for him. She could write him a long letter once she got home, telling him how much she'd enjoyed her time with him, wishing him all the best with Annie as his bride.

Sarah moved about the boys' room, finding their garments, glad that she'd washed their clothes the day before so that most—if not all—were clean. She packed the twins' shared suitcase, leaving out only their nightshirts. If they didn't get too dirty this afternoon, they could wear the same shirt and pants that they had on today. When she was done, she went downstairs to help prepare supper.

The family soon joined them for the evening meal. The twins and Josie's two sons were excitedly relaying the events of their day. "…And we got to play on the swings at the *schuulhaus*," Timothy said. Jacob had taken the four boys with his three youngest brothers to the schoolyard at the edge of the property to play on the swing sets.

When the boys were done with their tale, Emma informed them that tomorrow morning they'd be leaving Happiness.

The twins were upset. "We'll never see Elam and Will again!" Timothy cried.

"*Ja, ya* will," Emma assured them. "They are

your cousins. They'll come visit you, and one day you can come back for a visit."

Josie smiled at each twin. "This isn't *gut*-bye for always."

Sarah's young brothers looked sad until William distracted them with ice cream.

The next morning, Sarah was packing the last of her belongings when Ellen came into the room and sat on the bed. "Breakfast is ready," she said.

Sarah shut her valise and offered a small smile. "Did you help your *Mam* this morning?" she asked.

Ellen nodded. She was quiet a moment. "Sarah, I'm sorry to see you leave. I liked sharing my room with you."

"And I liked staying here with you." Sarah thought back on the time she'd spent fixing Ellen's hair, tying her apron strings, sharing stories of Delaware and teaching the young girl how to bake Sarah's favorite recipes.

"Sarah! Ellen! Breakfast!" Josie called up from downstairs.

"Coming!" Sarah gave Ellen a hug. "I'd like you to come for a visit. I think you'll enjoy meeting my *mam* and *dat,* and my brothers Ervin and Toby."

"I'd like that." Ellen pushed off the bed and headed toward the door. "I wish you didn't have to leave."

Sarah picked up her valise and followed close behind. "I do, too."

"Will you come back for a visit?" the young girl asked.

"If I can." As she descended the stairs, Sarah thought of her mother and her duties at home. She had been away a long time. She wondered if her family could ever manage without her. She set her valise next to her brothers' suitcase near the door.

Moments later, when she entered the kitchen, everyone was seated at the dining table. Plates of muffins and rolls with platters of eggs and ham and bacon covered the surface. There was a gallon of orange juice and a pot of tea. Josie had also made fresh coffee, and the rich aroma competed with the delicious scent of bacon and freshly baked goods.

Sarah enjoyed her last meal with her cousins. She was sad to go and especially saddened by the knowledge that she'd never again see Jedidiah Lapp.

"I put my valise beside the door near the boys' suitcase," Sarah said after the boys had left for one last romp outside with their cousins.

Emma frowned. "Why did you do that?"

"Where else would you have me put it?"

Josie poured Sarah another cup of tea. "How about upstairs, where it—and you—belong?"

"I don't understand." Sarah enjoyed the warmth of her teacup as she cradled it with her hands.

"Sarah, you're not coming with us," her sister said. "I thought you understood that I'm taking the twins to Ohio for a couple of weeks."

"Ohio?" Sarah echoed, wondering if she was hearing correctly.

"Josie thought—and I agree—that you should stay here. In Happiness." Emma spread butter over a piece of toast. "Sarah, I had no idea how hard you had to work while *Mam* was ill. I think you should remain and enjoy yourself. Josie loves having you, and I think that maybe you're not unwilling to stay."

"I love it here," she confessed. "I do miss *Mam* and *Dat* and Ervin and Toby, but Happiness also seems like home to me."

"Then stay. *Dat* will send for you when he wants you to come home," Emma said. "Until then, you can help Josie here and take every moment you can just being a young woman without the extra burden of too much responsibility."

"I love *Mam* and *Dat*. I'd do anything for them," Sarah said.

"*Ja*, I know. And they appreciate all you've done. Without the boys to disturb her rest, *Mam* will be fine without you. You'll have enough to do once you are home again."

Sarah blinked back tears. "Are you sure it's all right?"

"I wouldn't have it any other way," Josie told her with a smile.

"Emma?" Sarah watched her sister closely.

"Stay. Enjoy your life, Sissy. Make a memory of every moment to last you a lifetime."

"I'll unpack," she said after she helped clear the table and wash the breakfast dishes. Her heart felt light. She would see Jed again. "When I come down, I'll do the laundry."

When Sarah returned, however, Emma, James and the twins were outside waiting to say goodbye. A car was parked near the front door. The travelers' suitcases were already in the trunk.

"Give me a hug, you rascals," Sarah told her brothers. The boys obliged by running into her arms and hugging her tightly.

"We'll miss you, Sissy," Timothy said, his light blue eyes overly bright.

"Lots and lots," Thomas added.

"I'll see you again soon." Sarah released them and ruffled their hair. "Where are your hats?"

"I've got them." Emma approached with a small black-banded straw hat in each hand. She set one on each little red-haired boy's head. "Give your cousins a hug," she instructed.

As the boys obeyed, Emma approached Sarah. "I love you, Sissy."

Sarah sniffed. "I love you." She hesitated. "Are you sure you want to take them?"

Emma smiled. "Do you mean because trouble follows them everywhere and Jed won't be around to rescue them?"

"They can be a handful," Sarah warned. She

watched as the boys ran about the yard, giving chase after Elam and Will.

"I'll manage." Emma paused and looked regretful as she studied her sister. "Sarah, I'm sorry I wasn't there to help with *Mam.*"

Sarah waved away Emma's concerns. "It's fine, Emma. Don't you worry. *Mam* didn't want you to know."

"I realize that, but it wasn't fair to you."

"You were newly married. *Mam* wanted you to have a chance at happiness."

"What about your happiness?"

"Mam needed my help," Sarah said simply. "I'm happy."

Emma shook her head. "*Nee,* but you'll be happy one day." She grabbed Sarah in for a hug. Rounding up the boys, she and James saw the children seated in the backseat of the car between them.

"Bye, Sissy!" the boys cried out the open window.

"Be *gut* for Emma!" Sarah called back. She lifted her hand to wave. "Love you!"

She watched as the driver of the hired car drove down the lane and off the property before she went inside to help Josie with the morning chores.

Jed rapped on the door to the teacher's cottage until Rachel opened it. "Jed!" she greeted with a smile. "What a nice surprise!" She suddenly frowned as she saw his troubled expression. "What's wrong?"

"They left, Rachel!" Jed exclaimed. "Sarah and the twins! Gone with their sister, Emma. I didn't even have a chance to say goodbye! I needed to talk to Sarah. There is so much I wanted to say, but it's too late because she's gone!"

"Jed—"

"Is Noah here? I have to ask him if he saw them. I don't know how long ago they left. Jacob thought he saw the twins in a car early this morning—" He felt ill. He couldn't believe he wouldn't see Sarah again.

"Jed." Rachel's voice was calm, her smile serene, as she stepped aside, allowing Jed a glimpse of the kitchen.

Jed felt a jolt. Seated at the table sat Sarah, who met his startled gaze with a surprised look of her own.

"Sarah." He rushed past Rachel and into the room. "Why are you here? I thought you had left. Are the twins here? What about Emma and James— did they leave or stay?" Eager to learn more, Jed fired one question after another until Rachel began to laugh at him.

"Sit down, Jed," she urged, "and give Sarah a chance to answer."

Sarah, who had stood when Jed entered, sat down again. "Emma took the twins to Ohio. I'm staying with Josie and William for a while."

Jed sat close to her. "Praise be to God!" he whispered, his heart filled with gladness. He was pleased to see Sarah's blue gaze brighten.

"Why not have a seat and a cup of coffee?" Noah suggested with wry humor.

Jed glanced at him and grinned. "*Ja,* I'd like some coffee." He sat down next to Sarah.

A cup was set before him. A plate was pushed in his direction but he was too busy gazing at Sarah to pay any attention to anything else. Noah cleared his throat, finally drawing Jed's attention.

Jed looked at his brother, who stood, his expression unreadable, with his arm about his wife. He stared at them a moment. "What's going on?"

"Do you want to tell him or should I?" Noah asked.

Rachel leaned into her husband. "You tell him."

Jed narrowed his gaze. "What is it? Is something wrong?"

"*Nee,* Jedidiah," Noah said, his warm brown eyes sparkling, his lips curving upward. "Rachel and I are going to have a baby."

Jed blinked. "A baby?" He jumped up from his seat, grinning from ear to ear. "Congratulations!" He hugged Rachel and then slapped Noah on the back before he gave in and hugged him, too. "When is the happy event?"

"April," Rachel said. "Or March—we're not exactly sure yet."

Chuckling as he studied the parents-to-be, Jed resumed his seat next to Sarah. "I'm happy for you." He studied Rachel carefully. He wondered how Rachel's accident would affect her pregnancy. "You will take care of yourself?"

Rachel inclined her head, her expression turning serious. "I'll be watched closely."

Sarah was silent as she watched him digest the news of his upcoming niece or nephew's birth. "Will you continue to teach school?" she asked her friend quietly.

"For a time, unless the doctor says differently. Eventually, we'll have to find someone to take my place." Rachel cradled her abdomen, as if her touch could somehow protect her child and ensure a safe birth.

"Who?" Jed asked.

Rachel smiled when Noah's hand covered hers on top of her belly. "I haven't given it much thought, but my cousin Nancy would be a *gut* teacher, if she wants the position."

"That's an excellent idea." Jed studied his surroundings—the warm, cozy kitchen with its whitewashed walls and cabinets. He thought of the rest of the house—the bedroom, bathroom, living room and pantry that he'd helped to build. He thought of his own house, the one he wanted to build for Sarah. "You'll need a house. We'll have to find you property."

Noah looked startled. "*Ja,* I suppose we will."

"Nancy lives nearby." Rachel stood to heat water on the stove. "She won't need the cottage right away. She may want it eventually, but we'll be able to stay after the baby is born." She reached into a cabinet for the box of tea bags.

Jed became caught up in the excitement of Rachel and Noah's news as the morning lengthened. Sarah's presence was the highlight of his day, and his sister-in-law's pregnancy had increased his joy.

"I should get back," Sarah declared after a time. "I promised Josie I'd do laundry." She rose from her chair. "I didn't expect to be gone this long."

Jed stood. "I'll take you home." To his delight, she accepted his invitation. "The wagon is outside."

Rachel and Noah followed them out of the cottage. Sarah hugged Rachel and Noah and waited while Jed congratulated each one again.

"Sarah, I'm glad you're staying," Rachel said. "Jed, it was *gut* of you to stop by." Her dark eyes twinkled as she flashed a look from Jed to Sarah.

"You don't know how glad I am to see you," he told Sarah as he helped her into the wagon. He climbed in the other side and faced her; he was in no hurry to go.

Sarah looked at him, her blue eyes glistening. "Early this morning, I thought I was leaving and that I'd never see you again, but then the Lord had other plans for me."

"Thanks be to God," he said softly. He captured her hand and laced his fingers through hers. Her touch warmed him and he felt an overwhelming tenderness for her.

God had chosen her for him; he was sure of it.

Chapter Eighteen

Jed didn't say a word as he steered the horse past his parents' driveway and down the road toward the William Mast farm.

Sarah wondered what he was thinking. He'd been upset when he thought she'd left for Delaware without telling him. Her world brightened. *He cares about me.*

Suddenly, he flashed her a glance and looked away again. "Sarah, could you be happy in Happiness?" He kept his gaze on the road as he waited for her reply.

Sarah saw the tension in his face and the hands holding the leathers. *"Ja,"* she confessed. "I could be happy here. Your village, your community, is aptly named. Everyone is caring and concerned for one another. Happiness has been like a second home."

"Sarah," he interrupted, "about the other day... when I took you to see my land"

She frowned. *"Ja?"*

"I didn't tell you everything about my plans."

Sarah braced herself. *"Ja,* I know," she said softly. "You plan to live there with Annie."

He pulled up on the leathers to stop the vehicle on the side of the road. "What did you say?" He studied her carefully, as if he were memorizing her features, imprinting each one lovingly into his mind.

She swallowed hard. "I know you plan to build a house and live on your land with Annie Zook," she said.

Jed shifted in his seat to face her fully. He placed his warm, firm hands gently on her shoulders. "I have no intention of living on that land with Annie. I have no intention—nor have I ever had any intention—of asking Annie Zook to marry me." He leaned in close so that his nose touched hers. She could feel his breath against her chin, her neck, and she felt a shiver of delight.

"I don't understand."

"It's simple, Sarah. How can I ask Annie to marry me when there is someone else in my life, in my heart, who I love more than anyone?"

Sarah placed a hand over her rapidly beating heart. "Who?"

"You," he whispered. "I love you, Sarah. I wanted you to see my land because it's *you* I want to spend the rest of my life with, *you* I want to build a house for and have children with, and love forever and ever."

Overwhelmed with emotion, Sarah felt her eyes fill with tears. "Oh, Jed, you know I'll have to go home eventually."

"We have today and tomorrow and each day after that, until that happens." He narrowed his gaze as if trying to read her thoughts. She must have worn her heart on her sleeve, because he shot her a smile so full of happiness and love that Sarah caught her breath.

"I love you, Jedidiah."

"I was hoping you'd admit it," he teased.

Sarah chuckled until the look in his eyes made her stop and stare. "I want all the things that you do," she said gently, "but I can't stay and neglect my family." She was torn between her desire to stay and her need to be there for her *mam* and family.

"I'm not asking you to."

"What are we going to do?"

"We'll enjoy every moment we can together." He paused and frowned. "I have this job to do. I can't avoid it. When it's done, I'll have enough money to make that last land payment."

"*Ja,* you must finish the work," Sarah said. Knowing that Jed loved her the way she loved him would make those moments apart from him bearable.

He took her hand and cradled it between his palms. "Will you allow me to court you?"

Her throat felt tight. "I may only be here a short time."

"How long?" Jed furrowed his brow.

"Two weeks? A month?"

His expression brightened. "Long enough for me to court you," he declared.

"But when it's time to leave—"

He shook his head as if denying the moment when she would have to return to Delaware. "Then I will go with you."

Stunned by his declaration, Sarah could only stare at him.

He looked alarmed by her silence. "Sarah—"

She cried out and leaned in to hug him hard before pulling back quickly. "I will be happy to be courted by you."

He was grinning from ear to ear as she sat back in her seat. "*Gut!* You've made me a happy man."

"Jed, we should keep our courting secret," she suggested, "at least, for now. Until we know what will happen…when I'll have to go."

Jed didn't look too happy about it, but he agreed. "I will spend as much time as I can with you. Will you allow that?"

Sarah grinned and wrinkled her nose at him. "Just let anyone try to keep us apart," she said, which seemed to please him immensely.

Sarah was feeling happy and excited as Jed pulled the buggy onto the road again. He had to return to the farm; she had to get back to help Josie.

He pulled into the William Mast barnyard and then turned to study her. "I'll see you again soon," he promised.

Emboldened by the knowledge of his love, Sarah dared to reach out and run her fingers along his jaw. She saw his eyes gleam a moment before she smiled and withdrew her touch. "I'll look forward to it."

He came around to the other side of the buggy and helped her to alight. "Think of me," he whispered.

"As if I can do anything else," she whispered, and then she waved as he got into the buggy and steered the horse back the way they'd come.

Sarah was feeling giddy as she entered the house and then the kitchen.

"Sarah?" Josie called as she came down the stairs from the second story. "Is that you?"

"*Ja,* Josie! Are *ya* ready for me to do the wash?"

Josie came around the corner from the steps toward the back of the house, where Sarah stood near the linen chest. "Did you have a nice visit with Rachel?"

Sarah went to grab Josie's armload of sheets. "*Ja.* Noah was there, and Jed stopped by for a visit." She hoped there was nothing in her expression or tone to give away what had transpired between them.

"Jedidiah Lapp just happened to stop by, eh," Josie said, watching her closely.

Sarah blushed and looked away.

"He's sweet on you, and you on him. He told you how he feels, didn't he?"

Sarah flashed her a startled glance. "I—"

"I knew it! I've known all along how the two of you felt about each other. I told Emma so, and she agreed. She saw it, too."

Horrified by how transparent she must be, she could only gape at her cousin. "Oh, dear. Does everyone know?"

Josie gestured Sarah toward the kitchen. "*Nee*. Emma saw only because I told her. I saw it because I've come to know you well. Jedidiah is a fine man, Sarah. I am happy that the two of you care for each other."

"I care for him a great deal."

Josie's lips twitched. "You love him."

Sarah released a sharp breath. "*Ja*."

She set the sheets on the table a moment and turned to plead with Josie. "Please don't say a word to anyone. I have to go home soon, and I don't know what is going to happen."

"You're meant to be together," Josie insisted. She grabbed the laundry from the table and carried it to the washing machine. "Emma and I felt you should stay here in Happiness to decide what you want for your life. If it's Jed Lapp, then all the better."

Sarah followed Josie to the gas-powered washer, measured out the laundry detergent and dumped the soap into the basin as the machine filled with water.

"I know that I love him, and he says he loves me, but we want to keep our relationship a secret for a while." Sarah touched Josie's arm. "Can you do that for me? Keep this secret?"

Josie chuckled. "I've kept it thus far, haven't I? And I knew it before you did."

Sarah felt herself relax. *"Danki,"* she whispered.

"No need. This is the way of the good Lord. Thank Him. I believe He has *gut* things ahead for you."

Sarah enjoyed every moment in Jed's company. He worked during the day, but come early evening, he managed to get away to meet her at the edge of the Mast farm. Once there, they would walk together, talking about their hopes and dreams, pausing from time to time to gaze into each other's eyes and smile.

The first week went by quickly. Sarah was happy to see the start of another week with no letter or telephone message from Delaware calling her home.

On Saturday, Jed took her again to see his property. This time Sarah was able to envision a house. Her home with Jed.

She began to spend more time at the Samuel Lapp farm and Jed came often to invite Sarah to dinner or supper, or to play games with his family. Nothing was said about Sarah's presence; no one seemed to care whether or not they were courting, or that it might seem unusual for her to be with the Lapps almost as much as she was at William and Josie's.

"Sarah." Jed's soft voice interrupted her thoughts. He was driving her home after a shared meal with his family. "I thought we'd spend time with your cousins tomorrow."

Sarah looked at him. "That sounds like a *gut* idea. You don't mind?"

Jed frowned. "Why should I mind? They are your family. I want to spend time with them. We've been spending more time with my family lately. I don't want Josie and William to feel slighted that we haven't spent as much time with them."

"I don't think Josie feels slighted," she said. In fact, Sarah knew differently. Josie was always eager to hear what activity she and Jed had engaged in that day. Sarah, eager to share her happiness, obliged by telling her cousin about her time with Jed—at least, the things she felt she could tell. She didn't tell her how they held hands as they took a stroll, how they sat close in the buggy with shoulders touching but nothing else. The contact of shoulder against shoulder was Sarah's greatest delight next to simply being in Jed's company.

After two and a half weeks of pure bliss for

Sarah, a letter arrived. Jedidiah, who had come to visit, was there when the mailman stopped to drop off the mail. Thinking that he would save the Masts a hike to the box, he had carried the stack of mail directly to the house. He'd had no idea that there was a letter among them for Sarah from Kent County, Delaware—from her father.

Josie flipped through the pile of mail and handed the envelope to Sarah. Her brow furrowed with concern when Sarah paled as she accepted the letter and tore open the seal.

Sarah unfolded the page. Her heart thumped hard as she read her father's script. Her eyes begin to sting with the fresh onslaught of tears. She looked up, closed her eyelids and whispered, *"Nee."*

"What's wrong?" Jed studied the woman he loved and was immediately concerned. She looked unhappy and almost physically ill. "Is it your *mam?*"

"'Tis from *Dat,*" she said. "He wants me to come home." With letter in hand, she hugged herself with her arms.

"Sarah—" Josie began and then stopped. "Jed, why don't you take Sarah outside? The boys aren't about. You can sit on the front porch and talk."

Jed nodded. He needed to know what the letter said. He'd promised to go with her when she had to leave, but he had work to finish first; he would have to follow her as soon as he was able.

He led Sarah onto the front porch and saw her

comfortably seated in a rocking chair. "May I see?" he asked her gently. He extended a hand toward her.

Silently, she handed him the letter. He began to read and felt a crushing blow that the time had come for Sarah to go home when he couldn't immediately accompany her.

"Sarah, I have this job to finish, but I'll come as soon as I can."

She looked at him, her expression bleak. "Jed, I understand if you don't want to come—"

"Sarah Jane Mast," he said, having recently learned her middle name, "I'm coming to Delaware whether you believe it or not. I love you and I'm not about to lose you."

Sarah's lips quivered. "I love you, too." She stared out into the yard. "What if *Mam* has taken a turn for the worse? What if she needs me? What if something has happened and we can't be together—ever?"

Jed stood before her and gazed lovingly into her eyes. "I will come, and nothing will keep us apart. We will face whatever we need to face—together. *I love you.* Do you understand?"

Sarah nodded and her gaze brightened while a tiny smile curved her sweet lips. "*Ja,* Jed. I understand."

Chapter Nineteen

Mid-August, Kent County, Delaware

The sight of her parents' home warmed her, then gave her a little chill. She climbed from the car, grabbed her valise and thanked the hired *Englischer* driver for the ride. Ervin and *Dat* came out of the house as she approached.

"Sarah!" The cry came from her father, who hurried down the porch steps.

Sarah met him halfway and launched herself into her father's arms. "*Dat!* It's been so long."

"Over two months." He hugged her tightly and she closed her eyes, recalling all those times he'd held her when she was a little girl.

Ervin stood behind their father, waiting to greet his sister. "Sissy," he said. "You're looking well. Happiness seems to have agreed with you."

Sarah gave her brother a hug and then stepped

back and regarded them both worriedly. "How's *Mam?*" She trembled at the thought that her mother had become ill again.

"Why don't *ya* go inside and see for yourself?" *Dat* picked up her suitcase, and following her hurried steps, he carried it into the house.

Ervin lagged behind until he saw his brother Tobias exiting the barn.

"Sarah's home," she heard him call out as she entered the house.

She heard Toby ask, "Where is she?"

"Gone inside to see *Mam*."

Aware of her brothers as they entered the house behind her, Sarah rushed toward the room her parents had used as their bedroom since *Mam* became too ill to climb stairs.

"Daughter," Daniel said. "Where are *ya* going?"

Sarah frowned as she turned toward her father. "To see *Mam*."

"Well, you'd be going the wrong way. Your mother is upstairs. I imagine she's waiting to see you."

Sarah raced up the steps and into the room that originally had been her parents' bedroom. She entered the chamber, expecting to see her mother in bed with her face pale, her hair dull and her eyes listless. Stunned by what she saw, she paused on the threshold, unable to believe her gaze. Her mother looked the perfect image of good health. She stood near the bed, sorting and folding laundry. She didn't seem to notice Sarah's arrival.

"Mam."

Her mother turned, her eyes clear and bright, her color good, looking ten years younger than when Sarah had last seen her. Sarah stopped and stared. *"Mam?"*

"Ja, Sarah." She opened her arms, and suddenly Sarah was being held. Her mother's hug was firm and strong, and Sarah could scarcely believe it as she stepped back and examined her mother carefully.

"You look wonderful," she whispered.

"I feel it," *Mam* admitted.

Sarah was glad to see her mother looking so well, but she wondered with some guilt why *Dat* sent the urgent message to come home.

"Are the twins home yet?"

"Nee," her mother said. "They will be home later in the week. I wanted this special time with you."

Sarah grinned; she was glad to see her mother even if she missed Jed with every fiber of her being.

Sarah thoroughly enjoyed her mother's company as a week went by, after which her twin brothers finally returned home. Thomas and Timothy burst into the house like a whirlwind of boyish energy.

"Mam! Sissy!" they cried early one morning after they'd run out to the barn. "We've got a new calf!"

They were happy to be home to see their mother back to her former self. "Please come see!"

Together Sarah and her mother hurried out to the barn to witness the miracle that had occurred during the night.

"She looks like a fine young heifer," her mother proclaimed upon studying the newborn.

"She?" Thomas eyed the animal with a scowl. "How come Betsy didn't have a boy cow?"

"Don't *ya* mean a baby bull?" Timothy said with a grimace at his brother.

"Any calf is a miracle of life," their mother told them gently. "I'm sure this young one won't be the only offspring Betsy gives us."

"*Ja,* Thomas," Timothy told his brother. "Look how many offspring *Mam* had."

Sarah tried to control her amusement, but she couldn't hold back a chuckle. "You're absolutely correct, Timothy," she said after she managed to become serious again. "*Mam* had six of us."

"*Mam?*" Thomas asked. "Do you think Betsy will give us six calves next time?"

"*Nee*, son," Ruth said. "Just one at a time."

A week passed and then two without a phone message or a letter from Jed. Sarah began to worry that Jed had changed his mind about coming to Delaware. Had he decided that he didn't want her?

Sarah recalled their moments together, the laughter they'd shared, Jed's smiling eyes, his profession of love for her.

Please, Lord, don't let him stop loving me!

She went about her day, trying to be cheerful, and she must have succeeded, as no one said a word. No one seemed to realize that while she was smiling on the outside, she was crying inside. Every morning and afternoon she stood at her bedroom window and stared out toward the road, praying for him to appear.

But he didn't. Finally she headed downstairs to keep her mind busy by doing chores. She worked harder and took on more chores than she did when *Mam* was ill, until one morning, her mother called Sarah into her parents' bedroom.

"Sarah," *Mam* urged softly, "sit down here on the bed by me."

Sarah obeyed and looked at her mother in question.

"Something is wrong," *Mam* said. "What is it, child? What's bothering you?"

Sarah remained silent, as she suddenly had to fight back tears. "I love you, and I love being home, but…"

"But what?" Ruth encouraged softly.

"I miss Happiness, *Mam*," she admitted, looking away. "I miss him."

"Jed?" Her mother's soft query gave Sarah a jolt as she spun to meet Ruth's gaze.

"You know about Jed?"

"I may have heard about him from Emma and Josie, but mostly, I suspected that there was something special between you from the first moment I saw the two of you here in Delaware before he went home. I couldn't know that he lived in Happiness or that you'd see him again, but when I heard that he did and that you were spending time with him, I knew."

"Oh, *Mam…*" Sarah allowed her tears to fall. "It's been over two weeks, and I haven't heard a word from him. He said he would come, but he hasn't. I thought he would call or write, but I've had no message and received no letter."

Ruth smiled and stood. "Stay there, Sarah." She knelt by the bed and rummaged beneath until she withdrew a large white cardboard box. Setting the box on the bed, she sat and shifted it to rest between them.

Sarah gasped as she saw the powder-blue dress inside the box.

"Your wedding dress." Ruth smiled as she lifted the garment for Sarah to see. There was also a cape and apron and a new prayer *kapp.*

Tears filled Sarah's eyes as she gazed at it. *"Mam…"*

"I made it while I was recovering." Ruth laid the dress across the bed quilt.

"I wonder if I'll ever get to wear it." Sarah

touched the fabric. It was a dress that any young bride would love to wear.

"You'll wear it," *Mam* assured her.

Sarah hoped her mother was right and that someday she'd wear the dress. She wanted to wear it for Jed.

That afternoon, a dark car pulled into the barnyard. Sarah exited the house in time to see Jedidiah step out of the front seat of the vehicle.

"Jed!" Sarah rushed to his side. She studied him, drinking her fill of the wonderful sight of him.

Jed grinned. "Sarah. I told you I would come."

And Sarah felt her world brighten. Suddenly, *Mam, Dat* and her older brothers exited the house and surrounded her and Jed.

"Jed! 'Tis *gut* to see you again. Welcome!" *Dat* beamed at him.

"Sarah was just saying how much she loves and misses you," her mother said, and Sarah blushed.

"She did?" Jed's expression softened as he looked at Sarah with love.

"Jedidiah!" a young voice cried, echoed by another, as the twins ran from the back of the house.

A car door opened, drawing everyone's attention, and Katie and Samuel Lapp stepped out from the backseat.

"Ruth. Daniel. I'd like you to meet my *vadder* and *mudder*—Katie and Samuel Lapp. *Mam. Dat.* Meet Ruth and Daniel Mast, Sarah's parents."

"We're pleased to finally meet you," Samuel said.

"I wondered if this day would ever come," Katie said with a teasing twinkle as she met Ruth's gaze. "My poor son has been miserable without her."

"*Ja,* Sarah, too, has been unhappy without Jed."

Jed edged toward Sarah and captured her hand, despite being surrounded by family. Sarah was too happy to be embarrassed. Jed had come, which meant that he still loved her. *Thank the Lord!*

Sarah left Jed's side to hug Katie and then Samuel, who looked pleased by the attention.

"Welcome to our home." Ruth smiled and gestured for all to come inside.

Sarah studied *Mam* and Jed's mother, noting how comfortable they were with each other, as if they hadn't just met, but were lifelong friends. Everyone took a seat at the long kitchen trestle table, and with Sarah's help, Ruth began to pull muffins and cookies from a shelf in the pantry. Katie put on a pot of water for tea. Sarah smiled to see her moving about her mother's kitchen, looking as if she were at home.

"Sarah, the reason my parents are here is to meet yours. I wanted your family to know mine, since we'll all be family soon." Jed paused. "I spoke with Ruth and Daniel," he continued. "I asked permission to marry you, and—"

"We happily gave it," Ruth finished for him. "Josie wrote me often while you were in Happiness, telling us how she thought it was between the two of you. Your sister, Emma, confirmed it."

Daniel rubbed his bearded chin. "Learning how much you mean to each other made giving our blessing an easy decision for us."

"Jed was unhappy during the weeks after you left. We could see how much he loves you," Katie told Sarah. "We knew you were the woman God has chosen for him."

"It was plain how much Sarah loves Jedidiah," Daniel said.

Samuel smiled. "So it looks like there will be a wedding."

Sarah beamed at everyone happily. Suddenly, she grew quiet. "But where will we live?"

"Jed has land in Happiness. A bride should reside in the house her husband provides for her." Ruth poured a cup of tea for Katie. "You and Jed can come for visits. We want you to be happy, and if that means living with Jed in Happiness, Pennsylvania, then we are content."

Ruth and Daniel exchanged meaningful glances. "Now that I am well again, I'm allowed to travel," her mother went on. "There is no reason why we can't come to visit you."

Sarah was moved to happy tears.

"Now that is settled." Jed rose and extended a hand to her. Sarah took hold of his hand and allowed him to lead her outside.

"This is real," Sarah breathed when they stopped and gazed into each other's eyes. "'Tis truly happening."

"*Ja,* this is real," Jed murmured. The adoring look he gave her made Sarah inhale sharply. His smile was tender. "I love you, Sarah."

"I love you, Jedidiah. I was so afraid that you wouldn't come—that you'd changed your mind about me."

"Never," Jed said huskily. "I will love you until my last breath and beyond. We are meant to be together. I prayed for a forever love, and the Lord gave me you."

"It began with twin boys who ran out into the parking lot and a handsome young man who saved them," Sarah said. "And then I was blessed by God again when I visited my cousins in Happiness, Pennsylvania, and found him...*you.*"

Jed reached out, drew Sarah into his arms and simply held her. Sarah could hear the soft inhalation and exhalation of his breath. His nearness, his scent and the strength of his presence were all she'd ever wanted and more.

It seemed that Jed didn't want to let her go, and Sarah loved being within the circle of his arms. But then he released her and gazed into her eyes. He ran a finger along the front edge of her prayer *kapp.* "I've never felt this happy." His voice was low, husky.

"I feel the same way." Sarah gazed up at him, stared at his mouth, his nose, the warmth of his beautiful light brown eyes.

"Let's go inside. Our families are waiting for us."

And holding hands until they reached the front porch, they entered the house and noisy kitchen where their families talked of wedding plans and of joyous things to come.

Epilogue

Six months later...

Jed and Sarah prepared for company. They'd moved into their new home two months ago after marrying in Kent County, Delaware, during the first part of November, with another wedding celebration with their Happiness community a week later. Soon after, their Happiness church community came together to construct the newlyweds' house on the land that Jed had purchased from William and Josie Mast and had paid for in full.

Katie, Samuel and their other children, including Noah and Rachel, who was beginning to get large with child, arrived in time for supper. Moments later, a car drove up, bringing the Daniel Masts from Delaware for a visit.

Sarah felt Jed's hand on her shoulder as she opened the door to her family. *"Mam! Dat!"* She grinned at her brothers—all four of them. "Welcome to Happiness, Pennsylvania!"

"Did you have a *gut* trip?" Jed asked.

"*Ja,* the travel was fine," Daniel said.

"Come in!" Sarah urged. "Come in!"

As the Daniel Mast family entered the house and greeted the Samuel Lapps, Jed and Sarah exchanged loving glances.

"I thank the Lord for the day that He brought me to Happiness—and to you," Sarah whispered.

Jed bent his head, kissed his wife, and then with his arm around her shoulders, he moved inside and into the noisy household filled with family.

He paused in the hallway to touch Sarah's face, and then with his wife close to his side, he shut the door, locking in the warmth and love, and embracing the wonder of God's many blessings as they returned to enjoy the gift of their extended family.

* * * * *

Dear Reader,

Welcome back to the Amish village of Happiness in Lancaster County, Pennsylvania. Happiness is a place I love to visit time and again. This community is home to warm, caring and giving people. I first shared a glimpse into the Happiness Amish world with Noah Lapp and Rachel Hostetler's love story. Now Noah's older brother Jedidiah searches for a love like Noah and Rachel's. In *Jedidiah's Bride,* Jed travels to Delaware to help his uncle sell items at a local flea market in Dover. There he meets Sarah Mast, a young woman who has shouldered a tremendous amount of responsibility since her mother became ill. From their brief time together in Kent County, Delaware, to their surprising reunion at a Lancaster County farm, Jed and Sarah will explore their hopes and dreams as their friendship develops.

Jedidiah's Bride is a tale of selflessness, responsibility and commitment. Sarah's love for her mother and her commitment to caring for her parent in her time of need threatens to keep Sarah from realizing her dreams. But as God will reward us for our sacrifices and commitment to love here on earth, family sometimes understands and rewards a loved one's sacrifice.

As you look around at the lovely wonders of the

spring season, think of Sarah and Jedidiah…and God's plan for them and all of us. Sometimes, when we need something, we simply should pray to God. After all, He created us—and who better knows what is right and good for us all.

God bless,
Rebecca Kertz

Questions for Discussion

1. How and where did Sarah Mast meet Jedidiah Lapp? Did you notice anything special about their meeting? Do you think God had a plan when the two met?

2. Sarah was sent away with her brothers to her cousins in Pennsylvania. Why didn't she want to go? Do you think she had a good reason for feeling this way? Did she make the correct choice?

3. How did Sarah feel once she reached Lancaster County? What surprised her most about her stay?

4. Sarah Mast and Rachel Lapp became fast friends. Why? Did they share something in common? Have you ever met someone who became a fast friend? If so, why do you think that happened?

5. What happened between Jedidiah Lapp and Annie Zook? Why did they end their relationship? Do you think Jedidiah made the right decision? What influenced his decision?

6. Sarah was away from her home in Delaware for a long time. Were you surprised by that and by how she felt about Happiness, Pennsylvania? Why do you think she felt this way?

7. Throughout the story, Sarah and Jed each prayed to the Lord to help them when they needed Him. Do they believe they prayed for the right things? Or do you believe that God listens to all our special intentions and is there for whenever we need Him?

8. Sarah was a little upset to learn that her sister, Emma, had visited their parents before coming to Happiness and didn't tell her. Was that a normal reaction for Sarah to have? Why do you think she acted this way?

9. When she was called home, Sarah left for Delaware without Jedidiah. She was happy that her mother was doing well, but a little upset that she'd been called in a hurry as if there was an emergency. Do you believe Sarah only felt like this because she wasn't ready to leave? And why wasn't she ready?

10. Do you feel that Sarah and Jedidiah will be happy together? Will they have a good mar-

riage? What made Sarah entrust her heart to Jedidiah? What convinced Jedidiah that Sarah was God's chosen wife for him?

LARGER-PRINT BOOKS!

GET 2 FREE LARGER-PRINT NOVELS PLUS 2 FREE MYSTERY GIFTS

Love Inspired®
SUSPENSE
RIVETING INSPIRATIONAL ROMANCE

Larger-print novels are now available...